THE KEEPER'S BATTALION

THE KEEPER ARCHIVES BOOK THREE

S. T. SANCHEZ

Cover and title design by Meghan Edwards
Edited by Courtney Johansson

ISBN 978-1-959872-00-9

www.thepamperedcatpress.net

Books by S. T. SANCHEZ

The Keeper Archives

The Portal Keeper
The Secret of the Realms

The Sunwalker Trilogy

Sunwalker

Nightwalker

Darkwalker

For

Katherine Armstrong Walters, my dear friend and fellow author. Thank you so much for telling me about your publisher. I wouldn't be on this adventure if I hadn't sent them an email.

Chapter I

Ajax

It still felt like a nightmare, one Ajax hoped to wake up from, but Blake's fallen expression dissuaded any doubts that Ajax had. The forest remained still and silent as if mourning the loss of Niv's bright soul.

Striker, the leader of the elves, continued to pound against them, blow after blow. Each time Ajax thought they took a step in the right direction, the evil elf had beaten them back two paces. Now chaos filled the kingdom. Striker had followed Ajax and his friends through the portal, a magical entrance between two worlds that Ajax himself had been tasked to guard.

To make things worse, Ajax was the one who had made it possible for the portal to be accessed from Striker's world. The elf leader had come to the kingdom of Rastella with his army, catching everyone off guard. He slaughtered men, women, and children. How many casualties had befallen the kingdom? No one knew. They hadn't even had time to bury their dead properly.

Ajax and Blake thought they had rescued all the prisoners and were well on their way to taking back control of the kingdom when Striker had turned the tables on them yet again.

This time he abducted Nivara, Ajax's best friend and the prince's betrothed, leaving behind a ransom note of sorts. But instead of gold, Striker had a list of demands. If they didn't complete them in time, her life would be forfeit.

The first demand had been met immediately. Striker had left two lackeys behind at the portal entrance. Before the soldiers left this world, they demanded Ajax's medallion, an enchanted pendant infused with magical blood from his ancestors. It magnified his powers, making them much easier to access and it had a defense mechanism built in that caused the medallion to protect him in times of need.

Ajax took solace in the fact that the medallion ceased calling his name. When separated from it in the past, the amulet would call to him, growing louder as the distance between them increased. Ajax didn't understand why he couldn't hear the call now but remained grateful. It had almost driven him mad the first time the voice started talking in his head.

"Your Highness, we need to go. The others need to be apprised of the situation. Your father needs to restore order to the kingdom, and I need to seek council from Sliver," Ajax said, shaking Blake from his thoughts.

When they had first found out about Nivara's abduction, Blake wanted to follow her immediately. Ajax had to use physical force to restrain him from passing back into the other world. For one thing, the portal resided in the middle of an endless chasm in the other realm, or rather, the bridge connecting the realms, as Sliver had explained it. They had traveled back through the portal to Rastella on dragons. If they entered now, Ajax and Blake would plummet to their deaths. Ajax racked his brain trying to figure out how Striker had done it. Ajax had thought himself to be quite smart when he moved the portal to that location. But it had not been clever enough.

The second reason Ajax didn't want to travel through the portal had to do with Striker's demands. The elf leader desired to trade Nivara for an elixir of invincibility. The Maxwell son would have thought this impossible, if he, Blake, and the king hadn't found papers referencing this potion in a secret room hidden inside the castle. It required three ingredients: a mystical glowing flower located in the deepest abyss in the Mer Realm, a unicorn hair, and a dragon eggshell.

Not having the slightest idea of where to find any of these items, Ajax hoped Sliver could assist them. Ajax had just become aware of how much the universe encompassed. Sliver, the seer and dragon who had been training Ajax, had just recently informed him of the existence of other realms. Three existed in total. The world where he had met the seer didn't even rank as a realm officially, but acted as more of a waystation between the worlds.

It still boggled his mind. There had been no time to process any of this new information. Ajax hoped Sliver could shed some light on these new developments. Ajax reached his hand forward and pulled Blake to his feet. He had never seen the prince look so powerless. Desperation reflected in his eyes as he took Ajax's hand.

"We have to get her back," he choked out in a half sob.

"Don't worry. We will. But we must be strategic about this. We won't be doing her any favors if we rush into this and underestimate Striker again. He won't kill her," Ajax added in a tone he hoped reassured Blake. "He wants his potion too much to risk that."

"There's a lot people can live through," Blake said sullenly.

"I won't rest until we bring her home safely," Sky vowed. He shifted into his smaller size, scurried up Blake's leg, and leapt onto his shoulder. "Niv's tough and smart. Who knows, by the time we get there, she may have already escaped," Sky added with a wink.

Sky, the first creature Nivara had come across when she entered the portal, continued to hold up better than Ajax had anticipated. As a cambriar, a shapeshifting creature, he could change into any animal. However, he could only transform into each animal one time and once he had transitioned, he could never revert to that creature again. At present, he resided in the form of a hoosula, a small ferret-like animal with extra skin under his arms, which helped him to soar between trees. He was also very, very blue.

"You're right." Blake nodded in agreement. "If anyone can outthink the elves it would be Nivara. But let's not waste a second, just in case."

A light snow fell as they hurried back towards the Maxwells' homestead. They had divided the prisoners they rescued from the castle into two locations, Ajax's home and Nivara's. The king, at present, resided at the Maxwells' along with most of the others. Ajax still didn't know what had become of Sam, the new portal keeper, and Leif, Striker's son, the elf who had risked everything to save them from his father. Ajax prayed that they returned safely to his home.

As Ajax cracked open the door to his house, jovial conversations greeted him. His cozy home felt overcrowded but no one appeared to mind. Not having enough seating for everyone, many people sat crisscrossed on the floor. Blankets and pillows lined the living area floor, adding to the comfort of those not afforded a chair.

His brother looked overjoyed. It had been a long wait for Axel to be reunited with his family. Axel leaned with his back up against the hearth. Veda sat on his lap, her head leaning against his chest, eyes closed. Even in her sleep, Axel's daughter looked content. Next to Ajax's brother stood Edwin, Axel's son, and their father's namesake. Sinda, Axel's wife, sat on the other side, leaning over her son's head and resting hers on Axel's shoulder.

Seeing them reunited reminded Ajax that good things could still happen. They had been parted too long. The king had taken most of the visitors from the other world, or at least the ones he knew about, and imprisoned them over the past few months. His fear and prejudice had clouded his judgment. The queen had finally released them after some slight threatening on Sliver's part. Ajax hoped Blake's parents would start opening their minds and hearts to these new friends once they saw them for the non-threatening beings they were.

Mother Maxwell busied herself in the kitchen, preparing a soup of some sort. Their biggest pot sat steaming on the stove as Neely, another creature from the portal, chopped vegetables and herbs and his mother mixed and tasted, adding herbs and seasoning as she saw fit.

It warmed Ajax's heart to see how easily his mother had made friends with these unique beings. Neely had a sweet disposition and a striking beauty too, but her dark, hollow eyes could startle anyone who had never seen a mermaid before.

The king and queen sat at the kitchen table. They conversed in hushed tones but stopped when they saw Ajax enter. Blake followed behind him, looking disheveled and hopeless. Sky leapt off of Blake's shoulder and scampered through the countless bodies, looking undoubtedly for his best friend Leif.

"Where's Nivara?" the queen asked, craning her neck to try to see behind the boys.

"She's gone," Blake answered, unable to meet his mother's eyes.

"The elves have taken her," Ajax said. "They have given us a list of demands to meet if we ever want to see her again." He turned and surveyed the room. "Where is everyone?"

He assumed Sam and Leif had made it back in one piece since the queen had been delivered in safety.

"I'm not sure where everyone disappeared to, but I'm sure they will be back soon," the king said. "Sliver wanted to make sure all the elves are gone before we return and start to work on rebuilding the kingdom."

"Let's go find them. We need to leave at once," Blake said, looking panicked.

Ajax pressed his hand on the prince's shoulder. "Sliver will be back soon. And we don't even know where the others went. We can't rush this. It's too important." Then he craned his neck around, looking for Sky. "We need to wait for Sky to get back too. He must be searching for Leif. We should eat and rest while we can. We all want Nivara back, but there are things we need here first."

"How can you eat at a time like this?" Blake balked as Ajax walked into the kitchen.

His mother ladled some soup into a bowl for him and handed him a loaf of bread.

"Blake, this isn't going to be over in a day. We are going to need our sleep. I'm as anxious as you are to get Niv back, but we need to plan. We ought to counsel together with everyone. I need to go back to the keeper archives and do some research. I can't imagine we shall be ready to return through the portal any sooner than a couple of days."

Ajax set the bread on the table and pressed the bowl of soup into Blake's hands.

"A couple of days?" Blake asked, his tone incredulous.

"You're going back through the portal?" the queen asked, her eyes wide in astonishment. "But Blake will stay here."

Blake took a reluctant seat at the table and set the soup in front of him.

"Of course I'm going back," Blake insisted.

"But the elves are gone. Niv might not even be alive." She reached her hand out to touch her son's hand but he recoiled from it.

"She's alive," he said firmly.

"The elves left and we should just rebuild and find a way to destroy the portal. We barely survived this invasion." The queen's eyes welled up with tears. "I can't risk losing you. It shall be more dangerous going to their land. They will have the upper hand."

Blake opened his mouth to argue, but the king spoke before he had a chance to utter a word.

"Of course he has to go after Nivara. He'd never forgive himself if something happened to her." The king squeezed his wife's hand tenderly. "Do you think I wouldn't go if you had been taken in her stead?"

Tears ran down the queen's face. Mother Maxwell found a clean handkerchief and gave it to Blake's mother.

"When the others have returned, we shall counsel together." The king looked to Ajax. "Like we ought to have done from the beginning. We will get Nivara back. But Ajax is right, we need to be smart about it. Gather intel. Make a plan."

Mother Maxwell brought bowls of soup for the others. They ate in silence, turning at every sound, hoping for the quick return of their friends.

Sky beat Sliver back to the Maxwell homestead. He brought Niko, a giant talking rhino; Sam, the new portal keeper; and Leif, an elf and Sky's best friend, with him. Ajax gave them a brief update as they waited for the dragon to return. It surprised him that Sky hadn't filled them in on anything yet, but Leif said Sky just insisted they hurry back.

He described to them how two elves had been waiting for them at the portal, and how they had arrived too late to stop them from taking Nivara from their world. Ajax explained the loss of his medallion and Lord Striker's demands for them to gather the ingredients for the invincibility potion and deliver him the final product.

Shock and awe were reflected in the eyes of his family and friends.

"But if you give him the potion, how will he ever be stopped?" Edwin, Ajax's father, asked, leaning forward on his elbow. "He wiped the floor with us already and he could still be killed."

"We'll have to think of something. Some way to imprison him or switch the vial at the last minute..." Ajax shrugged, unsure of the solution, when the door to his home opened, startling the group.

Sliver, at last, arrived home.

"You're back," Neely said.

"Is the castle empty?" the king asked.

Sliver reported that the castle had in fact been abandoned, which Ajax knew to be true. Striker took what he wanted, and what he still needed, he knew would be delivered to him in due time. Ajax would find a way to deliver the elixir.

Ajax and Blake quickly filled Sliver in on the events at the portal. "Sliver, why is my medallion silent?" Ajax asked.

"Because you are no longer in the same world," Sliver said. "Even magic has its limits. I will teach you how to remove that bit of magic before you re-enter the portal."

"Is that why I can't contact Niv?" Ajax asked, trying to contain his hope, but feeling relieved even before the seer could answer.

"I believe so. It makes the most sense. Telepathy is another form of magic."

"She's not dead." Ajax felt the tension release from him. He had been able to reach Nivara through their telepathic link when she remained in Rastella. But the link had stopped working. Sam, the new portal keeper, had suggested that perhaps the connection had ceased because Nivara died. Leif argued that his father needed Nivara and wouldn't have gone through the trouble of taking her just to kill her. As much as Leif's logic had made sense to Ajax, he still had no valid reason as to why their link had been severed. But now he did. He shared a relieved look with Blake.

"If you thought her dead, then why go after her?" Mother Maxwell asked, looking confused.

Ajax glanced around the room and saw a similar look on the faces of his father and the queen.

"Because she's not dead," Blake answered fiercely.

"Because I wasn't certain. I didn't want to believe it, but hearing this from Sliver just confirms it," Ajax said.

"So, can we hurry up and make a plan? I can't just sit here and do nothing." Blake looked to the others; desperation filled his eyes.

"Yes, now that everyone is caught up, it's time to make a plan to rescue Nivara," Sky agreed.

CHAPTER II

Nivara

Many questions should have been floating through Nivara's mind, but the one that kept coming to her foremost thoughts was "When had this elf last bathed?"

The putrid smell made her want to vomit. Nivara had been flung over his shoulder for the last half hour, placing her nose too close to his armpit and the stench that emulated from it. She'd been counting the minutes until he would set her down and she could breathe again at last.

A whistle rang through the air and Niv's wish became reality as hundreds of elves came to a halt. The elf carrying her dumped her on the ground, the hot sand burning through her pants.

Niv bit her lip, deciding then and there that she would not cry out in pain. She pulled her knees up to her chest to limit her contact with the scorching earth.

The sand continued as far as she could see with no sign of any vegetation in sight. No clouds flitted through the sky, offering no shade to help alleviate any of the heat. The elven army made any thoughts of escape improbable. She'd never make it past all of them.

Her hands and feet throbbed under the tight ropes that bound her. She rubbed at the red marks forming beneath the bands. They felt tender to the touch and would be much worse by the end of the day.

The blazing heat beat down on her as she glanced around her surroundings. Niv used her sleeve to wipe the sweat from her face. However, in mere moments perspiration covered her face again. What she wouldn't give for some shade.

"Five minutes," she heard an elf, who looked like he might have some authority, call out. He had a red sash wrapped around his waist and the other elves deferred to him. "Water and a quick bite, then we must continue. Lord Striker wants us back by midday tomorrow."

Back where? Niv wondered.

As soldiers all around her guzzled down water, Niv's mouth ached for even a drop. Seeing them eating dried meat and cheese in front of her didn't even bother her. But she'd give almost anything for a swallow of water.

Breathing in the fresh air, she took a moment to be grateful for her change of scenery even if it would just last another few minutes. Anything to keep her mind off the soldiers and their waterskins.

Hundreds of elves surrounded her, all tired and grumpy. Perhaps if they stopped for a longer rest, the elves would forget about her in their rush to get home. But she knew the hope to be a feeble one. At least Nivara hadn't set eyes on Striker for several hours.

Closing her eyes, Niv focused on Ajax, reaching out to him with her mind and calling to him like she had done before.

Silence.

Why wasn't it working anymore? They had conversed multiple times telepathically. Perhaps something in this world kept her messages from reaching him.

But it mattered little. As much as she might like to chat with her childhood friend, Niv knew beyond a doubt that Blake and Ajax would come for her. No matter how long it took, they'd never give up on her. She just needed to survive until then.

CHAPTER III

Blake

The room was crowded, but for once the smallness of the Maxwell house wasn't Blake's focus. Instead he looked around the den and marveled at the friends he had, friends willing to do whatever it took to get Nivara back.

Axel and Sinda sat side by side, hands intertwined, waiting for Blake to speak. Niko sat beside them, followed by Neely, Sam, and Leif, concerned expressions staring back at him. Sky sat perched in Sam's lap, relaxed as ever, enjoying a back rub, even amid all this chaos. Sliver sat behind Blake with Ajax, while Blake's parents sat with the Maxwells at the kitchen table listening.

"You've all heard Striker's demands," Blake said. He could hear the desperation in his voice but didn't care. "We've got to find the ingredients for the elixir, make it, and deliver it to him as soon as possible. We should leave tomorrow."

To Blake's astonishment Sliver spoke against him. "That won't be possible."

"What?" Blake asked, still unable to believe what he had heard. "Niv could be getting tortured as we speak." He ran a hand through his hair in frustration.

"I see several problems," Sliver said, standing from his chair. "One problem is the time distortion that happens when anyone travels through the portal. We could be months or even years apart from Nivara if we simply stroll through. It is unpredictable. I believe it is a spell. One I need to look at unraveling. We need to make time pass the same between all the realms."

Blake slumped his shoulders in defeat. As much as he wanted to take off into the portal, Sliver had a point.

"Another problem is that you need the shell of a dragon egg. There are some in this world, but they are not close. It would take a few days to get there on foot."

"We also need to study the keeper archives," Ajax interjected, not bothering to stand as Sliver had done. "The portals to the other realms remain hidden. They are mentioned in some of the text I saw. Perhaps there is information about the other realms as well. It would be wise to know a little about the worlds that we will be entering."

"All right." Blake threw his hands up exasperated. "Sliver, you fly me to the dragon eggs and Ajax can do research in the meantime. But as soon as we get the shell I am leaving."

Sliver set his hand gently on the prince's shoulder. "I feel it might be more prudent for me to accompany Ajax to the archives. The sooner I figure out the time spell, the better. I can direct you to the place where the dragon eggshells are. But only one of you shall be able to see them."

"Sam?" Blake guessed. After all, as a portal keeper like Ajax, she should have received a cloak made from the same magical material as the Maxwell son's cloak.

Sliver shook his head and turned towards the kitchen.

"Edwin, it has to be you."

"Me?" Father Maxwell balked. "I don't have magic like my son." He turned to his wife, looking for confirmation.

"It is in your blood. You never had the medallion to help you activate it. With time and work you could learn to develop and access it. But seeing magic is far easier. Since my blood runs through your veins, you just need to wear your cloak and I can help nudge the magic awake in your veins enough for you to see what's there. The cloak is made from dragon scales, which also possess magical qualities. Wearing it, you will be able to see things no one else can. Sam cannot because the dragon that bonded with her bloodline is dead. There is not enough magic in her blood to do anything."

The room fell silent as everyone stared at Edwin. Mother Maxwell squeezed his hand.

"Is it dangerous?" she asked.

"There is danger in breathing. Every day we live is a gift. No one can know everything, not even an old seer like me."

His words didn't console Ajax's mother.

"But for all that, I believe the danger is minimal," Sliver added. "However, you know the dangers that lurk in your forests and mountains better than me."

Edwin looked to his wife; her eyes teared up but she gave him a small nod.

"I'll go. I still don't know if I shall be able to do anything, but if I can offer any aid in this mission to save Niv, I'll do it."

"I appreciate your assistance," Blake said.

"I'll come too," Sky said as he nuzzled into Sam's stroking hand. "Anything sounds better than looking through dusty books."

"I would be happy to accompany you also," Leif echoed.

The king cleared his throat and rose from his chair. "It looks like we have the beginning of a plan. Tomorrow Blake and his companions will ride in search of dragon eggs. Sliver and Ajax shall begin research, and the queen and I will start trying to rebuild the kingdom. It is a daunting job—Striker destroyed so much in such a scant amount of time." He shook his head sadly. "I'd like to leave now so we can get back to the castle before nightfall." The king offered his hand to his wife, helping her up, then turned his gaze toward Sam. "Sam…I mean…Samantha, could you go in the morning to Ni—" he stumbled over the word, "to find Thomas and the others recovering at his homestead? Let them know that I request all who are able to return to the castle. I'll need all –hands –on deck to aid with repairs and checking on the rest of the kingdom."

"Niko and I shall come in the morning to assist," Neely said from across the room.

It warmed Blake's heart to hear this offer of kindness after all they had endured at the hands of his father.

If her offer surprised Niko, his face didn't betray him.

"Yes, we are both fine carpenters. We will offer what assistance we can until Ajax re-enters the portal. At that time," he paused and looked to Neely, "I must part ways with everyone. I have an obligation to Spots and I must deliver his ashes to his family."

Spots had been the captain of the ship Neely and Niko worked. He had risked the wrath of the elves by assisting Ajax in their world. Spots ended up giving up his life trying to aid them by spying on the elves, and that ultimately led to his capture and death.

Blake admired Niko's loyalty.

"Thank you," Blake said, giving a quick nod to the rhino. "You have done more than our kingdom deserves after how we treated you."

Axel whispered something to his wife Sinda, and then stood. "Let me accompany you back to the castle," he said as the queen and king carefully moved through the crowded room towards the door. "It has been a long day, and I would feel better knowing you arrived back safely."

"How we ever doubted the Maxwells' loyalty…" the queen said, her voice cracking. "Never again," she added with more resolution.

After Axel and the king and queen had gone, Sliver turned back to the group.

"We should all rest and start the day fresh tomorrow, but first let me attend to the injuries you've acquired from battle with the elves. We will all need to be at our best for the tasks that loom before us."

"Take my room," Ajax offered.

Blake had almost forgotten about the injuries he had sustained while fighting the elves. His mind was focused on Nivara and getting her back left little room for any other thoughts.

One by one the dragon treated Leif, Sam, and then Blake, their injuries disappearing as each one emerged from the bedroom.

"That's the kind of magic I ought to be learning how to do," Ajax noted.

Blake felt exhausted, but he gave Ajax a halfhearted smile. "I think for now, I'd rather have the 'destruction-and-havoc-causing sorcerer' on my side."

After everyone had been attended to, the Maxwells did their best to bring in enough water for them to get cleaned up. No one took a full bath. Far too many people took refuge in this house at present for such luxuries. But Blake cleaned his face and neck and washed away the dried blood from the injuries he'd sustained while fighting. The dragon healed him, but some of the evidence still remained. Ajax gave him and Leif a clean shirt.

Once they'd all freshened up, Blake watched as Sliver pulled Edwin aside. He whispered something to Ajax's father, and Edwin disappeared into a room for a moment before returning with his cloak.

Edwin put the cloak on, and Sliver touched his shoulder and muttered something under his breath. Then he pointed to the cloak.

Edwin's eyes widened. He saw something extraordinary, something they could not see. Nothing looked any different to Blake. Of course, no magic had been awakened in his blood so he wouldn't have been able to see anything different.

The comfort of this bed did not equal the one Blake had become accustomed to back at the castle, but it didn't matter. His thoughts stayed focused on Nivara.

Blake tried to decline the offer to take Ajax's room, but even Mother Maxwell had insisted. He thought about going to the castle, but Leif, Edwin, and Sky would all be here and Sliver had yet to give him the map.

No, staying closer was the right choice. If questions arose about the map, he needed to make sure the answers could be acquired immediately. They didn't need another delay. He pulled the blanket up, tucking it under his chin.

His body felt fatigued, but his mind wouldn't stop. Sleep would not come tonight, nor anytime soon, but still he tried. Being exhausted would not help him save his betrothed.

CHAPTER IV

Nivara

Water. Food would be nice too, but if Niv could just get some water, she'd never complain again. She had no idea how many hours it had been since they passed through the portal. The elves had flown on langabeasts for a while but abandoned them when the animals grew tired. Nivara hadn't minded the ride, but the Pegasus-like creatures scared her with their sharp teeth and bright red eyes. Afterwards the elven army marched for hours, resting only once, and then continued marching again.

Dust covered her throat and tongue, making it hard to swallow. The heat beat down on her back and neck as they carried her across the vast desert. She could feel her skin burn but had no way to shift positions. As it grew dark, they entered a forest, offering Niv a reprieve from the heat as well as a change of position as she sat under a wide, leafy tree while the elves rested once more.

She'd first encountered Leif and Sky in a forest when she arrived in their world for the first time. Niv wondered if this was the same forest. Some of the vegetation looked familiar, but she supposed any forest here might have similar plant life.

"Here," a large elf grunted, thrusting a tan waterskin in her hand. His rotted black teeth showed between his lips as he sneered at her.

Her hands ached as she accepted the skin from him, wishing they would cut the binds off her wrists and ankles. Niv averted her eyes from the elf, trying not to wonder if this elf had drunk from the same waterskin.

The hot liquid ran down her throat, offering a small amount of relief to her dust sodden mouth. She sucked the skin dry too soon, wishing for more.

"Could I have some more, please?" Niv asked.

"Please?" The elf let out a long, obnoxious laugh, as if this had been the funniest thing he had ever heard. "Would you like me to cut you free too?" He slapped his knee. "You are lucky Striker wants you alive, or I would not have given you anything."

Niv glared at the elf. How could Leif be so different than the rest of his people? Her stomach rumbled, and the soldier looked at her as if waiting for her to ask for something else.

Then he pulled out a loaf of bread and ate it with slow deliberate bites in front of her.

Deciding she did not want to give him the satisfaction of him denying her anything a second time, Niv remained silent.

Tents sprung up in quick and efficient fashion as soldiers prepared meals and other elves patrolled the perimeter and set up a watch. Niv watched intently, hoping to learn as much as she could about the soldiers' routines in hopes of taking advantage of a lapse in planning, giving her a way to escape.

The wafting aroma of the food tortured her empty stomach. But Niv watched with keen eyes as the elves went about their business. She noticed several elves climbing trees and picking a green almost rectangular fruit of some sort.

Since the elves did not intend to feed her, she made it her mission to feed herself. Niv noticed that a few feet behind her grew a tree adorned with the same fruit. Several pieces had fallen from the branches and lay sprawled along the forest floor.

Some looked rotten as if they had fallen long ago, but many still looked green and bright.

As the darkness closed in, turning day into night, Niv shifted her body over in slow intervals until she reached one of the fruits. She snuck covert bites as the elves became drunk and less concerned with her.

The fruit exuded juice and had a nutty aftertaste. She finished three, quelling her hunger for the moment. Niv looked around for more, but no other trees grew in her vicinity. And she'd need to be much hungrier before she would be willing to try one of the half-rotten fruits. She knew it wouldn't be this easy all the time to procure food and wished she could have eaten more.

A cool breeze swept through the forest and Niv welcomed it. Although grateful for the shade and the coolness of the night, Niv still felt uncomfortable. Her clothing remained damp and coated in dirt and grime, and she felt sticky and dusty. A bath and a cold glass of water would do wonders. But for now, she'd content herself with fresh air and the little bit of solitude she had.

By the end of the evening, a large group of soldiers sat gathered around a roaring fire. A dark-haired elf watched Niv intently. It made her shudder. This soldier didn't look at her with the same disdain as the others, but his fixed glare unnerved her all the same.

Niv shifted her gaze from the elf and turned her thoughts back to home. Blake flooded her mind first as she leaned against a tree, trying to get comfortable. He must be sick with worry, and was probably blaming himself, but she hoped the others wouldn't let him. The fault lay at Striker's feet.

At least she had been the one taken. That consolation had to keep her going. Her friends and family remained safe. Niv just had to be patient; she knew where the portal lay and with time would figure out how to escape.

CHAPTER V

Sky

Sky started to seriously reconsider his decision to accompany Blake. The earliness of the hour at which Blake decided to depart had lessened the breakfast choices by a considerable amount.

Instead of the normal plates of pancakes, eggs, biscuits, and bacon, there had been apples, bread and butter, some dried meats, and hard cheese. Mother Maxwell placed the leftovers in Leif's, Blake's, and Edwin's travel bags. So lunch and dinner would be even less appealing.

If he had chosen to accompany Ajax to the archives instead, at least delicious meals would have interrupted the boring day of study.

Still, they were on the road now. The action of moving towards one of their objectives would make the time pass by faster and get them a step closer to rescuing Nivara.

He wondered how she fared. Lord Striker made torture an artform. And although Sky did not believe that Striker would resort to killing Niv and losing his leverage, he didn't want to imagine what Nivara could live through.

Blake and Edwin rode side by side in the front on two of the castle steeds that Luka, a stable hand, helped rescue from a fire that Sky had started to distract the elves in a rescue mission. Luka had been one of the Rastellians rescued but he had also helped save the horses in the process. Leif rode behind them on a white stallion, who bristled at the slow pace. The horse neighed and reared his head back, trying to break free of Leif's steady grasp. Sky, in his smallest size, sat perched on the elf's shoulder.

The snow on the road made a thin covering, making it easy for the horses to keep a steady pace.

In two days' time they should arrive at the foot of the Silvan Mountains, barring no sudden snowstorms. Then they would hike an hour or so to find a concealed cave where the dragon eggs resided.

Sliver had explained that just as some lizards shed their skin, dragon eggs shed their outer layer of shell from time to time, giving fresh nutrients to the embryo inside. Only Edwin would be able to see through the powerful magical façade that Sliver had placed over the eggs and this location. At least, they hoped so. Edwin had not appeared very confident at first, but since Sliver had helped awaken the magic inside his blood, Sky could see Edwin beginning to believe.

Edwin wore the cloak he received when he became the portal keeper. As he rode, Edwin kept looking at it and feeling it between his fingers in amazement. Ajax had explained to Sky that although the cloth looks like ordinary fabric to everyone else, once the magic is awakened inside someone, they see dragon scales.

It still looked like an ordinary cloak to Sky, but he hoped that Edwin now saw dragon scales in place of fabric. If not, then their entire journey to the Silvan Mountains would amount to nothing more than a colossal waste of time.

"Is it time to eat yet?" Sky asked, looking in front of him and seeing nothing but trees and a dirt road ahead.

A wry smile played at the corner of Leif's mouth. "If we stopped to eat as often as you would like we would never get anywhere," Leif said. "Ever," he added with a wink.

"Did you eat this much back in your world, or is it just my wife's cooking you enjoy so much?" Edwin called over his shoulder.

Blake shook his head. "That one never gets full. When this is over, we'll have to send him home before he bankrupts the castle coffers."

"Ha. Ha." Sky's tone didn't reveal a hint of humor. "Did you notice I shift into three different sizes? That takes a lot of energy. Feeding me is a small price to pay for my usefulness. My shifting sizes comes in handy, a fact that you are all eager to exploit if the need arises," Sky said in his defense.

Releasing one hand from the reins, Leif reached up and rubbed behind Sky's ears. "You know we are just teasing. You helped save all those prisoners in the barn."

"And saved Niv on the bridge," Blake interjected. "You're right, your ability to change has been invaluable."

At this time Sky didn't feel like he contributed much. Ajax had magic, Blake aided his parents in ruling a kingdom, and Leif's skill with a bow couldn't be matched. But hearing his friends' memories helped remind him that he played a part in all this too.

Nivara had a terrible fear of heights and had almost fallen off a nearly invisible bridge, but he had shifted into his largest form. Sky let Niv ride him like a horse to safety.

And only a couple of days ago, after shifting into his smallest size, Sky helped initiate a rescue plan that freed a large group of prisoners from Lord Striker.

Sky had been thinking a lot as of late about locking into this creature.

As a hoosula he could shift into three sizes. A large horse-like size, a ferret-like size and a cockroach-like size. The more Sky stayed in the body, the more he felt at home. But he just couldn't make the change permanent. Not yet.

Niv was gone. Captured! Probably being tortured this very moment, but he tried not to think about it. What would happen if he made the change permanent and then needed to shift to a different animal to save Niv?

He just couldn't do it. Not until Nivara returned safe and sound.

In his world he had pretty much run out of animals to turn into. But the enormous library in the castle had so many books on animals, Sky didn't know if he'd ever get through them all.

So now he had an arsenal of animals at his disposal. Some large, others small. Hundreds of animals he could shift into should the need arise.

As they journeyed on, the group fell into a comfortable silence and Sky took advantage of the quiet to nap on Leif's shoulder.

A gentle nudge awoke Sky. He yawned and stretched, arching his blue back up as far as he could.

"It is just past midday," Leif said, dismounting from his steed. "There is a small clear stream just ahead. We thought this would be a good place to stop and eat and let the horses rest."

Sky leaped from Leif's shoulder, shimmying into his midsize form as he glided towards the ground. By the time he landed, the change had completed.

"It's about time. I'm famished and parched, too."

The elf turned to his saddlebag and pulled out a waterskin, offering it to his friend.

Sky vehemently shook his head. "No, thank you. I will only drink that as a last resort. It tastes funny after sitting all day." He careened his head around. "You mentioned fresh water?"

"It's just over that hill. Blake and Edwin went to refill their skins."

Sky left Leif to attend to the horses and scampered up the small rise that the elf had motioned towards. Once at the top he could see Edwin sitting on a rock nibbling on some cheese, while Blake crouched with his waterskin. From his vantage point, Sky couldn't see the stream yet but assumed it ran along where the prince knelt.

The sun reflected off the snow, almost blinding Sky. He trotted forward and paused at the sound of a branch breaking. He turned, expecting to see Leif, and screamed.

"Ahhhh!" Sky yelled as he lunged to the side, avoiding a huge beast that pounced towards him. He scurried up the closest tree as fast as his legs could carry him. He paused on a branch but was startled to see the cat-like creature spring onto the trunk of the tree and pounce onto the branch just below him. The cat's bulky body didn't hinder his speed.

"Help!" Sky screamed as he soared from tree to tree in a frantic panic as he tried to avoid the creature.

W*here are my companions?* Sky thought, but the speed of the creature following him left him no time to even venture a glance.

Sky jumped towards the ground, hoping the monster behind him didn't like water. As he leapt towards the stream, he felt air whoosh by him as the giant cat-like creature swiped at him, just missing his hind legs.

"Over here!" Sky heard Edwin yell.

It's about time, Sky thought, frustrated at his friends' slow response.

He heard a thudding sound behind him, hoping arrows rained down on the beast. But the creature behind kept coming, a loud roar coming from him, making him sound even more ferocious.

Sky ran towards the stream and skidded to a halt. No, not a stream as Leif had believed, a river raged before him. The water moved in fast swirling currents with huge white rapids running down this stretch of the river.

Sky turned, panic overcoming him. The huge monster ran straight for him. The river looked to be his best option and he prayed that death by drowning would not be his fate.

Just as Sky braced himself to plunge into the river, Blake emerged in front of him. He stood panting, brandishing his sword. He must have run up the riverbank.

The cat monster leaped forward, his sharp teeth gleaming in the sunlight. Sky closed his eyes, unable to watch.

A second later he heard a thud; when he opened his eyes, he saw that the large cat had pounced on Blake.

"No!" Sky called out in alarm.

The creature moved, and Sky sighed in relief as it rolled off Blake, a large slit running down its abdomen.

"You're all right." Sky breathed in relief as Blake rose, blood dripping from his clothing.

"I'm fine. The blood is not mine." Blake kicked at the animal to ensure that it had in fact died, Sky thought.

At that moment Sky noticed an arrow protruding from its back. He looked up and saw Leif jogging towards him.

"Thanks for the assist," Blake said. "I don't think I've ever seen a mountain lion quite that big."

"I am just glad we finished it off before it devoured Sky."

Sky shivered at the thought of how close he had been to becoming lunch. "Me too. So that's a mountain lion. Let's hope it's alone."

"These mountains are full of bears, mountain lions, and snow leopards," Edwin panted, catching up to them at last. "You might want to stick close to one of us. These predators shy away from humans for the most part, but you're pretty much the ideal meal for these guys."

Sky shrank back into his smallest size and climbed back onto Leif's shoulder. "I'm not leaving this spot until we are back home."

Sky ate quickly, admonishing the others to do the same. His encounter with the mountain lion had shaken him to the core. He didn't think he'd ever been so scared in his life. His heart had almost pounded right out of his chest. Maybe his brother had the right idea after all. The appeal of Ajax's bedroom had enhanced tenfold.

CHAPTER VI

Ajax

It wasn't a surprise when Ajax arose and found Blake had already departed. He knew Niv consumed all Blake's thoughts. Ajax felt the same way, even if it didn't always show. But he had spent days in the dungeon with no food and a scant amount of water.

Ajax needed a little time to get his energy back and recharge. He would be no use to anyone if he collapsed. He too wanted to leave to find Niv as soon as possible. But Ajax had no idea where to find the portal to the Mer and Animal Realms. They had been mentioned in the papers in the archives. But Ajax had merely glanced at them before because of his haste.

Now every moment felt rushed. It felt like a guillotine hung over his head and any second it would crash down. He took his breakfast to go, cramming a few muffins and some apples in a satchel before hurrying outside to meet Sliver.

Ajax's eyes widened as Sliver stood before him in his true form, a majestic green dragon, with his wings outstretched. Most of the time he resided in the form of a human, a young man a few years older than Ajax with jet black hair and blue eyes.

"I thought we might fly today," Sliver said, winking at Ajax.

"Fly? You're not worried about scaring the townspeople?" he asked as he stepped closer, climbing onto the dragon's back.

"Many have seen me now. And my body aches to be in its true form. They shall learn soon enough they need not fear me. Besides, once we arrive, I will have to change back if I want to fit inside the library."

Once Ajax felt secure, the dragon leapt into the air, extending his wings, and flapping until they gained sufficient altitude to clear the trees.

The flight felt exhilarating, the wind rushing through Ajax's hair as the dragon sped forward. Nothing compared to the beauty of Rastella from this vantage point. He could see for miles in every direction. The snow-covered forest floors and babbling brooks painted a beautiful image. He wished everyone had the chance to see the world from this position.

It almost made him envious of Sky and his ability to shift into whatever creature he desired. Ajax wondered how much better it would feel to be the one flying as opposed to just riding. But Ajax liked being human too. Opposable thumbs let you do so much. Of course, Sliver could fly and look like a human so maybe he had the best of both worlds.

The flight ended too soon. Sliver flew at a much faster pace than Ajax's normal stroll to the castle.

Sliver landed inside the castle walls, startling a few soldiers and townsfolk who worked to clear away debris.

One soldier reached for his sword but stopped when he saw Ajax sliding down from the creature's back.

"It's all right," Ajax assured them. "He's here to aid us."

"He saved us from the elves, burned them to a crisp with his fiery breath," a young boy said with a look of awe and wonder in his eyes.

The dragon shifted into his human façade, causing a few of the people gathered to step back.

"Ah, if it isn't the brave young master Luka." Sliver gave the boy a warm smile.

Ajax remembered the lad now. He worked with Thomas, Niv's father, in the stables. Sliver and Sky had rescued a group of prisoners there. That must have been where Sliver and Luka met.

The king turned a corner and made his way forward after spotting Ajax and Sliver.

"Thank goodness you are here," the king said. "My wife told me that during my unfortunate accident," he mentioned, being gracious with his wording, "that you healed me. Please, we have many wounded. Many townspeople who escaped the initial slaughter hid, but not all made it out unscathed."

"Go and begin without me. I shall join you as soon as I am able," Sliver said before turning to follow the king.

The time spell would have to wait. Luckily, Blake would not witness this delay. Ajax knew Sliver could save the people of Rastella and could even help them heal without unnecessary pain. But Niv remained far from home and he wished for a moment that the king didn't know about Sliver's gifts.

Ajax felt a pang of guilt, prioritizing one life over another. They would save Nivara. And Sliver could still save the Rastellians. Both things could be accomplished.

The archives held the answers Ajax needed to rescue Niv. If he found the information fast enough, perhaps he could find the clues for fixing the time distortion of the portal too. If he could do both before Blake returned with the dragon eggshells, then no time would have been wasted.

Ajax noticed Niko and Neely carrying scraps of burned wood. He wondered if it came from the barn that Sky helped burn to the ground, but didn't waste any time stopping to ask them. He hurried off towards the library, happy to be working on something that would bring him closer to getting Nivara back.

How could so many books and scrolls fit in such a small room? Ajax had spent hours in the room searching through manuscripts. Thus far, he hadn't found much more than their original finding had informed him.

A piece of parchment lay in front of him with his notes scrawled out.

Mystical Glow Flower	Mer Realm
Unicorn Hair	Animal Realm
Dragon Eggshells	Silvan Mountains
Mer Portal	Never Ending Night
Animal Portal	Stinking Bogs

He hadn't found much to go on. Hopefully only one magical glowing flower existed in the Mer Realm. The unicorn hair seemed straightforward. But as far as the location of the portals, the scrolls only gave a region of the land where Leif and the others came from. Ajax knew nothing of the Stinking Bogs, except for the fact that it smelled. Blake had mentioned that when he traveled through Never Ending Night, he couldn't even see his hand in front of his face. How would they find a portal there?

Ajax combed through text after text, reading until his eyes burned.

Through the hours of searching Ajax did find a few interesting items. In a small leather-bound book, he found lists of all the spells placed on the library alcove—spells keeping papers from being burned or destroyed, spells helping to preserve the ancient texts, along with the spell that kept the books from leaving the room.

Ajax spent some time trying to alter the spell to allow him to bring texts out of the alcove. The small dusty room made him feel claustrophobic.

Ajax couldn't figure out how to lift the spell completely. But after working on it for some time he could expand the area the spell covered so that he could at least take things into the library.

After gathering armfuls of parchments, Ajax made his way to a large sunlit table in the library with a window looking out onto the castle grounds behind it. Just what he needed, a change in scenery.

Hours later Ajax hadn't found much. He'd gone through a stack of journals from his ancestors and a few from the Stonemans, but he found nothing related to time spells.

He flipped back to the page that contained the elixir of invincibility recipe. How could Ajax hand this potion over to an elf bent on the domination of the realms?

His eyes blurred looking over the page as he started to drift off to sleep. Ajax sat up straighter and rubbed his eyes, then noticed something he hadn't before. At the bottom of the page, he saw faint lines. He leaned closer to inspect the markings and found the faint markings to be letters.

Ajax couldn't decipher the language but he scrawled a copy of the message on his notes. Perhaps Sliver could decipher it.

Tin kuid vinkuro hors isto sol dur

He hoped it was an important note. Maybe it described how to counteract the elixir.

By the time Sliver arrived, he looked exhausted. Blood seeped through the seer's clothing. Ajax didn't realize Sliver's façade could get dirty.

"How's it looking out there?" Ajax asked as he rose and stretched, arching his back from the strain of sitting for so long hunched over old books.

"Better now, but I am feeling drained. I'm not sure how useful I'll be down here today." Sliver glanced around the library with an approving nod. "So, you figured out how to get books out of the tunnel. Any luck finding anything on time spells?" Sliver asked.

A large stack of books and manuscripts lay pushed to the side of the table. Ajax pointed to them.

"I've gone through a portion of them," Ajax answered in a tired tone. "I haven't found much about the elixir either. I have a general idea of where to find the other portals. But I couldn't find any information on the other realms or what to expect. And I found…" Ajax paused and pulled out his notes, showing the foreign line to Sliver. "Well, I think it's another language. Do you know it?"

After taking the parchment from Ajax, Sliver examined the words.

"Hmm." He stared at the words for a long time before speaking. "I think I have seen this language before," he said as he passed the paper back to Ajax. He scratched his chin. "I can't read it. But if my memory serves me, I believe it is a language of the Mer Realm."

"The Mer Realm?" Ajax asked, a hint of excitement in his voice. "Do you think Neely will be able to translate it?"

Sliver shrugged. "I'm not certain. Since they lost the ability to return to their realm, they may not have seen the need to continue with all their traditions. It's worth asking her."

CHAPTER VII

Blake

The horses trudged through the thick snow that blanketed the forest floor. Their painstakingly slow pace grated on Blake's nerves. Every moment he remained here in this realm, Striker could be beating, starving, or doing who knew what to Nivara.

It helped a little that he had a task to perform. Finding the dragon eggshells would put them one step closer to finding all the ingredients for the magical invincibility elixir and one step closer to procuring Niv's release. He just hoped Ajax would be prepared to leave when he returned.

Whether or not Ajax had found all the locations of the rest of the ingredients, Blake decided he needed to leave. He couldn't wait any longer. Hopefully, Sliver and Ajax would have everything in hand when they returned. Four days would have to be enough time, he would allow no more.

Handing over an invincibility potion to a psycho elf lord didn't seem like a wise idea either. But Niv's life mattered more than anything else to him. It killed Blake not knowing Niv's situation. Even if he could only bargain with Lord Striker to allow him to switch places with Nivara, he would. Blake would do anything he could to save her. Even if it meant he'd suffer in agony for the rest of his days.

The winter's daylight faded too fast for Blake. If Striker had abducted Nivara in the summer they'd have hours more of light to travel by.

They rode against wind. Blake shivered, pulling his coat tighter and ducking his head to keep the cold off his face.

"Blake, I think we'd better find a place to camp," Edwin called from behind. "We don't want to risk a horse hurting itself on an obstacle we can't see."

"All right," Blake relented with a heavy sigh. He knew Edwin had a point. And truth be told, he yearned for a blazing fire to warm his weary bones.

Leif scouted ahead and found a small rocky alcove that would keep most of the snow and wind off them.

They dismounted their horses and divided up tasks to set up camp. Blake tended the horses, while Edwin worked on starting a fire with some of the dry wood they had brought with them. Leif and Sky worked fast, preparing some type of soup to hang over the fire.

Jovial conversation flowed as the camp came together, but Blake didn't feel like joining in. He hung back, brushing the horses, and taking his time to remove the saddles and tack.

When the soup had finished cooking, the conversation ceased as the others dove into their portions with famished looks in their eyes. Blake joined the others to eat.

He didn't begrudge them their happiness, but somehow Blake felt like it would be a betrayal for him to enjoy anything while Niv sat imprisoned.

He ate, lost in his own thoughts. The hot soup sapped some of the cold from him. Feeling a little thawed, he found a rare dry spot of rock to spread out his bedroll.

"At first light I want to be ready to leave," he announced as he buried himself under his blankets.

"Of course," Leif agreed.

"We made excellent progress today. If the weather stays consistent, we ought to make it to the edge of the Silvan mountains by midday, giving us several hours of light to locate the dragon eggs," Edwin said.

"Splendid," Sky said. "The sooner we get back the better."

A howl sounded in the distance and Sky jumped, then ran and situated himself between Leif's and Edwin's bedrolls.

"As if giant cats aren't enough." Sky shivered, but Blake didn't think it had anything to do with the cold.

"Wolves should stay away from the fire," Blake said.

Sky didn't look convinced.

Before the sun had crested the hill, Blake had everyone up and preparing to leave. Today's breakfast consisted of bread and cheese. Wasting the light of the day with cooking didn't even cross Blake's mind.

"You're certain that you'll be able to see the dragon eggs?" Blake asked.

"For the last time, Your Highness," Edwin answered. "I am confident that if we find the right place, I will be able to see through the enchantment. Ajax said wearing his cloak makes it possible," Edwin explained, pulling on his own keeper's cloak.

"Don't worry," Sky said, bounding from Leif's shoulder to Edwin's. "We can do this. We'll get the dragon eggshells, return, and leave with Ajax to find the flower and unicorn hair. Then we'll trade with Striker, get Niv back and find a way to beat the elves, with or without an invincibility potion."

"But how do you beat someone that's invincible?" Blake asked, a hint of desperation in his voice.

"We shall throw him in the deepest pit and never let him out," Leif said.

"Or drop him in the cavern." Sky shrugged. "I mean, we don't know if there is even a bottom, maybe he'd fall indefinitely."

"Wouldn't that be fitting?" Edwin nodded. "Ultimate power, but nowhere to go and no way to stop."

After another hour of riding, the Silvan Mountain Range came into view. Blake had visited the mountains once in his youth, but his memory had faded over time. The mountains in front of him stretched as far as his eyes could see. How would they ever find a small concealed cave in that?

"It is beautiful," Leif noted as they rode closer.

The snowcapped mountains lay covered in pines, cedars, and other evergreen plant life.

"I'm supposed to find a cave in that?" Edwin asked, echoing Blake's sentiments.

"It will be fine; Sliver told me we needed to search the tallest mountain," Sky said.

By the time they reached the base of the mountains, the task felt overwhelming. Blake felt like an ant with the entire world looming up before him.

"Where do we even begin?" Blake asked uncertainly. "They all look tall from here."

"Let us tie up the horses and scout around. Look for something that looks like a path. Then we will head up to the top of the mountain and see if we can get a better look," Leif said as he hopped off his mount.

"I'd feel better if he had warned us a little," Edwin said as he followed Leif's lead, dismounting from his mare.

"Climbing up the mountain will take hours," Blake said, sounding defeated.

"Maybe I can get a better vantage point if I climb up a tree," Sky said, motioning to a tall tree that stood off from the others. "I can get a good line of sight from that one."

"Give it a try," Blake said.

Sky scampered over to the tree and climbed up. The tree narrowed the higher up he ascended and began to swing. He continued up at a slower pace.

"Be careful," Leif called from below.

Sky paused a few feet from the top when the trunk became too weak to hold his weight. He slid around, looking in all directions.

"I see it. One peak juts out higher than all the rest. It's just to the east of here." Sky hopped and glided down using the bigger branches for support.

"Are you certain?" Blake asked.

"Yes. I had a magnificent view."

They mounted their horses with haste and rode east. When they reached the mountain that Sky pointed out, they tied up the horses.

"I don't mind scouting, but I am not going off on my own," Sky said, his eyes shifting nervously.

"You can accompany me," Edwin said.

Sky leaped from his spot on the horse, nimbly landing on Edwin's shoulder.

Blake ran a hand through his hair, still astonished at the expanse before him. "All right, let's spread out, but make sure you stay in the line of sight of the others. Holler out if you spot anything that looks like a trail, or if you see a cave, Edwin," Blake said, and then added, "Just don't get lost. We can't afford wasting time looking for any of us."

"Sliver wanted to conceal this place, so I think perhaps we should go into the trees some and then start looking," Edwin suggested.

"Good idea," Leif said. "Let us all go in…what do you think, twenty paces?"

Blake nodded his agreement and made his way into the forest. The trees at the foot of the mountain grew more spread out. But as they progressed it became harder to see everyone.

The search continued in silence for the most part. Occasionally one of the groups would call another over to see if they had found a trail, but nothing came of any of the halts in the search.

"I think it's time for a snack," Sky called out after an hour or so.

Blake didn't want to stop, but he could tell the others felt disheartened at the lack of results and thought a quick break might help boost morale.

"Fine, but a quick one," Blake said.

Sky leapt down on a pile of pine needles. "Ow!" he said in an exaggerated tone.

"Are you okay?" Leif asked.

"Yes, I just didn't realize a rock lay beneath this." He brushed the needles off the spot where he landed with his paw, and gasped.

"What?" Blake asked as Edwin turned around to see what had caught Sky's attention.

"A dragon's footprint has been melted into this rock," Sky said, sounding excited for the first time since they had embarked on this quest.

"Dragons can melt rock?" Blake asked, rushing forward.

"Apparently so." Leif knelt, touching the stone. "This must be the right direction."

"Edwin, do you see anything?" Blake asked, feeling a glimmer of hope for the first time in a long while.

Edwin hurried over to the rock and looked around. "Not yet, but at least we have a direction."

They headed deeper up the mountain, stepping with care, looking for more stones or other signs that Sliver had been here.

After about ten more minutes of hiking, the group came across a trail. Faint but present.

They trekked through the mountains for a few more minutes and Edwin pointed. "A cave."

"Where?" Blake asked, looking around.

Leif and Sky turned and twisted, trying to find the entrance as well.

"I'll take it as a good sign that none of you can see it." Edwin laughed. "Just follow me."

The others followed as Edwin led them to what looked like a rock wall in the mountain.

Edwin stepped inside and disappeared. Blake reached forward with his hand and it went through the magical wall. "I don't think I'll ever get used to this." Blake said, remembering his time in the library when he followed Ajax through what appeared to be a solid wall. It had ended up leading them to the archives that generations of portal keepers kept.

One by one the others entered the cave. And just like before, once through the wall Blake could see the cave they entered.

"It's empty," Blake said, disappointment heavy.

"It's beautiful," Edwin said. His eyes lit up, filled with awe, but Blake couldn't see why.

Edwin knelt and put pinecones into his bag.

"Pinecones?" Blake asked, picking one up and turning it over in his hands.

"Is that what it looks like to you?" Edwin asked, sounding amazed.

Sky sniffed at one. "It smells like a pinecone."

"What do the dragon eggs look like?" Leif asked. "I just see a cave with a passage blocked by a landslide of rocks, and lots of pinecones scattered around the floor."

Rubbing his chin, Edwin turned. "I wish you could see this. They are beautiful. The eggs shine like…like starlight, or a rainbow of starlight. It's hard to describe it. I've never seen anything like it, and there are so many dragon eggs. Too many to count. This cavern continues further than I can see."

"When this is all over and Sliver comes back to take off the enchantment, I want to be here," Leif said. "I would very much like to see what you are seeing."

Blake touched Edwin's shoulder. "If you got what we came for, I suggest that we get out of here. Let's go home."

CHAPTER VIII

Nivara

Sleep evaded Niv that night. The root-laden forest floor did not provide the ideal comfort to which Nivara had become accustomed. Her muscles ached and despite the fruit she found the night before, her stomach growled and her throat ached for moisture. At least her clothes had dried.

To Niv's surprise, the elves packed up with a quick efficiency and started on their way. The dark-haired elf she had seen the previous night came and collected her.

"Today you'll be taken to Elf City. Just do whatever Lord Striker wants and things will be easier on you," he warned.

"I don't care what he does to me, I'll never help him." She pulled against the elf and spat in his face.

She braced herself for a slap across the face or a punch to her gut but received none. The elf looked stunned but just wiped his face and slung her over his shoulder. He made his way to a large white horse with wings.

At least this elf doesn't stink as much as the other one, Niv thought.

"Where are you taking her?" a soldier elf asked as he sauntered over, staring at Niv with disdain.

"Lord Striker wants her brought to him immediately," the dark-haired elf said.

"But—"

"You dare to question me?" the dark-haired elf asked, stepping forward aggressively.

The soldier's eyes dropped to the ground. "Of course not, Telkin. My apologies."

Telkin spun on his heal and threw Niv onto the front of the horse.

She tried to suck in a breath but couldn't. He had knocked the wind out of her, and it took her a few moments of gasping to feel like oxygen reached her lungs again.

Leaping on behind her, Telkin pulled the reins and nudged the langabeast into the sky.

It flapped its wings hard, making Nivara's hair blow to and fro. Once it crested the trees it soared forward, jolting Niv. She thought she might fall but felt Telkin place his hand on her back to steady her.

It felt repulsive. Niv wanted to shake his evil hand off her but refrained as she felt certain that action would result in a fall to her death.

The city must not have been far from their camp. Either that or the langabeast flew faster than Niv imagined because the flight didn't last long.

If Nivara hadn't been slung over the front, it might have been an enjoyable ride. The animal flew with a smooth grace.

Looking forward would have been a better view than looking down towards certain death. Niv spent most of the ride squeezing her eyes shut and imagining she rode on the ground instead of flying above it.

As they landed, Telkin whistled to another elf to come take his langabeast, and pulled Niv to her feet.

He shoved her forward and pushed her towards a building that resembled a castle. No other building in the city compared to its grandeur.

Telkin brought her to a room and pushed her onto the floor. She struggled back as best she could with her hands bound tight together.

The dark-haired elf pulled out a sharp blade from his belt and stalked toward her.

"Get away from me!" she shouted.

"Relax, I'm just going to cut your bindings."

Niv paused, and Telkin made no movement towards her. She raised her bound hands towards him and held her breath.

His knife cut through the ropes easily.

"Striker requests your presence—" Telkin began.

"I don't care what Striker wants," Niv said, trying to sound brave even if she didn't feel it.

"Look," Telkin said. "I can bring you to him like that. Or you can shower and change." He shrugged. "I really couldn't care less. But I don't know what his plans are for you. This may be the last time you get this offer."

He pointed to a plate of food and a jug of some type of liquid.

"Eat and change, or don't. Striker isn't expecting you this soon. I flew you here, so we got here faster than he anticipated."

"I bet it's poisoned," Niv said, eying the food with suspicion.

He huffed, walked to the table, and took a huge spoonful of the food and a slug from the jug. He wiped his mouth with the sleeve of his shirt.

"Satisfied?" he asked with a sneer.

"Why? Why do this for me? I'm just supposed to believe you're doing this out of the kindness of your heart?" Niv asked. "I mean you're an elf." She spat the last word.

Niv thought he looked hurt at her words, but when she looked up at him his cold, black, stony eyes stared back.

"Of course not." He stalked towards her and leaned forward, whispering in her ear. Niv froze, not knowing what to expect. "I want something from you," he hissed.

Glancing around the room, Niv pointed at herself. "Something from me? You realize I'm a prisoner. What could you want from me?" she asked.

"You'll see." He smiled, and Niv shuddered. "I'll be outside. You have half an hour, and don't waste your time looking for an exit. There isn't one."

Once Telkin had exited the room Niv sprang off the floor. He had told her no other exit existed, but she couldn't help looking for herself.

Despite her desire to stay defiant, Niv knew she needed to keep her energy up so she took the plate and inhaled the food as she surveyed the room, then chased it down with the fruity liquid from the jug. Once convinced that Telkin had told her the truth, she showered and changed, welcoming the hot water and soap. Showering and donning clean clothes helped Nivara prepare mentally. She needed to make smart decisions. Niv would refuse to assist Striker, no matter what he did to her. But she'd be wise and would accept what the elves offered her if it benefited her and aided in her escape.

Chapter IX

Ajax

Much to Ajax's dismay Neely could not read the foreign writing he had found on the papers in the keeper's archive.

"I'm sorry," Neely said, frowning as she scrutinized the paper again. "I wish I could decipher it, but it's just random letters to me."

"It's fine," Ajax said, feeling disappointed. Something in his gut told him that this line contained vital information. But then again, maybe he just wanted it to.

Handing an all-powerful elixir over to the lord of the elves was the last thing Ajax wanted to do. However, he couldn't see any way around it. Lord Striker had outsmarted Ajax and his friends at every turn.

"Neely, I've been trying to decide the best way to go about retrieving the remaining two ingredients...I mean, if Blake, my father, and the others come back with the dragon eggshell, that is."

She placed her hand on Ajax's shoulder. "Of course they will. And then we will go find the rest of the ingredients and bring Nivara home."

"I think we should split into teams. That way the retrieval shall go faster. But I'm not certain how we should divide up."

"I'm going to the Mer Realm. I have to see where I came from and maybe I can help once we get there."

Ajax laughed. "Yes, but you're the only easy one. Of course you'll go to that realm. I think I should go there too. I feel like this is important," Ajax said, pointing to the foreign words he had scrawled on his notepad. "And if Sliver is right, then the Mer Realm holds the answers."

"Sky might want to go to the Animal Realm. I'd say Niko too, but he has another important matter to take care of."

Spots. The ladybug captain who had rescued Ajax from Death Lake and had given his life trying to aid them. Ajax admired Niko's determination to bring Spots' remains home to his family. Spots deserved more. If they survived their dealings with Striker, Ajax vowed to do all he could to repay the debt he owed to Spots and to Spots' family.

"So you and I shall go the Mer Realm. I am certain Leif will want to go with Sky since the entrance is in the Stinking Bogs somewhere. Given what Sliver said, Leif may just find his mother there. Maybe Blake should accompany that group. If Leif reunites with his mother, he may not be ready to leave her so abruptly."

Ajax nodded. "That's sound thinking. Perhaps you can offer these suggestions to Prince Blake. We don't always see eye to eye and he might take the idea better coming from you. After all, you came up with it."

"All right," Neely agreed. "What about Sam, Sliver, and Axel?"

"They all need to stay here. I can't leave my family undefended. Sliver is still working on fixing the time spell on the portal, so all the realms pass time the same." Ajax looked around, making sure no ears could overhear them, then leaned forward and whispered, just to make certain. "Besides, Sliver has another task he may need to do."

"What?" Neely whispered, leaning forward.

"He may need to close the portal indefinitely. Sealing it shut may be the only way to keep Striker from returning. And not just to our realm—he may need to close all the realms. If Striker becomes invincible, we have to try to minimize the damage."

"Is it even possible?" Neely asked.

"It has to be. I know Sliver doesn't think it is. But I believe anything that can be done can be undone," Ajax said, trying to sound more confident than he felt.

"What about the creatures that live in the…what did Sliver call it?"

"A bridge between the realms. We will have to get as many of the inhabitants from your world out as we can. After the items are collected, when Blake and I go to get Nivara, you and the others shall have to evacuate those you can."

"And just abandon the rest? That's not a lot of time."

Rubbing a hand over his face, Ajax felt tired to his core. He could see no other way around this.

"Can you think of a better option? Do we let Striker take control of everything if we have the means of locking him in one place? We'd be stuck there too. I'm not saving myself and condemning others."

"This is just a last resort?" Neely asked.

"Yes," Ajax agreed. "I just can't leave without some type of contingency in place. Feel free to think of a better strategy. I am open to suggestions."

Neely sighed. "Okay, I agree, we need to save whoever we can save. But I'm not giving up on you figuring out a way to defeat Striker. If anyone can do it, it's you."

How could she have such faith in him? He had failed to stop Striker when he invaded Rastella, failed to stop him from taking Nivara, and failed in keeping Spots safe. How could he defeat someone who always stayed two steps ahead?

CHAPTER X

Nivara

Nervousness and dread filled Nivara as Telkin led her down a wide corridor towards a location where Striker waited. Thick stone walls surrounded her on either side with torches spaced out, providing a low glow of light. Guards flanked every doorway. Niv tried to stand tall and keep a stoic face, not letting her fear show through. She didn't relish the thought of pain or torture, but prayed she'd be able to withstand it, to survive it. She couldn't be weak.

The long hall extended further than Nivara could see. The polished stone floor reflected the torch light. It surprised her to see the cleanliness of the castle rivaled that of Blake's home in Rastella.

In Niv's mind, she pictured moats and dark, damp halls, like the ones in novels when the hero entered the villain's lair. As they made their way down the torch-lit corridor, Nivara did her best to memorize the layout of the castle. Any piece of information she acquired could mean all the difference if a moment for escape presented itself. They approached two gigantic doors with ornate, carvings that looked to be erected out of pure gold. Nivara ran her finger down the side of one and gasped in horror as she now stood close enough to make out the figures. Images of elves slaying every manner of creature in horrific ways had been etched into the doors. It disgusted her.

Two elven soldiers positioned on either side of the entrance stared at Nivara with such a loathing as she'd never seen before. How could they hate someone so much that they'd never even met? As Telkin brought Nivara before the entrance, the soldiers heaved the heavy doors open.

As the doors cracked open, Niv could see a throne room. Striker sat on the gaudiest throne Nivara had ever seen. Covered in diamonds, rubies, sapphires, and other rare gems, not an inch of the surface remained bare. It couldn't be comfortable to sit on.

The obsidian stone walls of the throne room shimmered. It made the room more foreboding, but Niv could still see beauty in it.

"Bring her to me," Striker demanded when he noticed Nivara and Telkin.

The dark-haired elf nudged her forward with more force than necessary.

Niv glared at him but made her way forward. Although terrified of what Striker had in store for her, she looked forward and held her head high. Nivara didn't want him to see her fear. She hoped to be able to maintain a strong façade that Leif's father would not be able to see through.

"So this is the key that will bring me all my heart's desires," Striker said, looking her up and down.

Nivara bit her lip. Striker had no heart, but she doubted announcing that fact would be beneficial to her current situation.

His eyes shifted to Telkin. "Keep her alive. Other than that, have fun with her. But keep her breathing. She's the thing that will keep the sorcerer in line. Once I have the elixir, I'll gut her like a pig for the second time."

His laugh sent shivers down Niv's spine. Leif's father had almost killed her when she had last been in this world. If it hadn't been for Ajax using so much magic it almost killed him, Striker would have finished her off with a second stab of his sword. Sliver had healed her once Ajax had rid the tower of elves. Striker would not get a second chance; she'd make certain of that. Somehow.

The dark-haired elf offered a bow to Striker before grabbing Nivara's arm and yanking her out of the room.

Telkin dragged Niv through twisting corridors and down flights of stone stairways that spiraled down into oblivion. He kept up a fast pace that made it impossible for Nivara to get an idea of the layout of the building.

"The dungeons never used to be this far below ground," Telkin commented as they reached the end of the steps.

Niv peered back the way they came. They descended so far down that she couldn't see the doorway they entered from.

"When your companion escaped, Striker had workers on constant shifts digging deeper and making the dungeons stronger than ever. There is no chance of escape now," he said, staring straight at her as if reading her thoughts.

"I don't believe that anything is inescapable," Niv said with defiance.

He shrugged. "I guess I'll let you be the judge of that after you see where we will be keeping you."

A dozen soldiers guarded the entrance to the cells. The corridor leading to the cells had a giant doorway, wider and taller than necessary by about three times. Niv wondered why they built it so big. Down the passageway Nivara could see that each cell had its own guard and equally oversized doors made from some type of metal.

What did they keep down here? Niv wondered.

"Call for the troll. I need a cell door opened," Telkin said to a soldier on his right.

The soldier nodded. "Of course, Captain," he said as he reached into his pocket and withdrew a silver whistle.

The soldier blew into it and a piercing sound erupted from it. Niv covered her ears with her hands and waited. She had never seen a troll before.

Nothing happened at first, but after a moment Nivara thought she felt a vibration beneath her feet. A loud sound boomed from down the corridor, further than she could see.

The walls trembled and the ground shook as something made its way towards them.

She took a step backwards, not knowing what to expect.

Her eyes widened in shock as the oversized creature came towards her. No wonder they constructed the doorways so large and the hall so wide. The doorway looked small next to the gigantic monster.

The troll stood twenty feet tall. Three yellow eyes that glowed in the darkness stared forward. The troll had stringy black hair tied behind its head and a sharp-toothed grin, revealing shiny white teeth. Niv couldn't tell the troll's gender. It wore a ragged shirt and pants that fit snuggly. The troll rippled with muscles. She imagined a flick from the giant hurling her across the room.

The soldier pointed to a cell, and the troll reached for the handle and pulled a large metal door open. The door had to be at least six feet deep.

No wonder they needed a troll to open it. Escaping through the door would not be possible, unless Niv could somehow find a way to call the troll, befriend it, and convince it to open the door and help her take out all the guards. All in all, that scenario seemed as unlikely as Telkin just letting her go.

Once opened, Telkin escorted Nivara into her cell. Then he turned and sent the guard away and had the troll shut the door with him still inside the cell.

Telkin turned and looked at Niv.

Scrambling backwards, Niv looked for something she could use for a weapon in the small cell.

"I can promise you this," she said, trying to sound more confident than she knew she looked, "you will not be having any *fun* with me."

CHAPTER XI

Blake

The ride back to the Maxwell home was uneventful. Blake slept some over the two day journey home, feeling a little relieved that they now carried a bag of dragon eggshells with them, bringing them one step closer to rescuing Nivara.

He pushed open the door to the Maxwell homestead without knocking, too eager to see if Ajax had found what they needed to leave Rastella and to set off on saving Nivara. If the others thought it rude, none mentioned it, nor would they dare to with him being the prince.

The people in the room bustled around, preparations for the upcoming journey in full swing. Blake noticed several satchels filled with provisions in one corner of the room. Bedrolls had been tied tight and rested against a wall next to a line of various weaponry: bows, spears, swords, and the like.

Ajax leaned over a map spread across the kitchen table, in deep conversation with Sliver and Neely. He didn't even notice when Blake entered.

"You're back," Mother Maxwell said, relief washing over her face as Blake stepped into the main living area followed by Edwin, Leif, and Sky.

"Mission accomplished," Edwin said, hefting up a small bag.

Sky bounded towards the table. "Anything left from breakfast?" he asked. "Dried meat and bread get a little bland after a while."

Mother Maxwell smiled wryly. ""I might be able to find you a little something. In fact, if what I find doesn't suit your needs, I'd be happy to whip up an entire new breakfast. You can't imagine my relief now that you're all back in one piece."

Sky leapt onto the kitchen counter as Edwin strode forward and gave his wife a kiss on the cheek. Then Mother Maxwell turned and pulled some sausages and biscuits out. Sky dug into them without even waiting for them to be reheated.

"Any problems?" Sliver asked, looking towards Blake.

"Other than a huge cat trying to eat me?" Sky exclaimed between bites.

Blake waved his hand. "Naught worth discussing. We succeeded in our task. That's what counts. Now, what I want to know is if you've figured out the time spell and when we can leave."

Neely bent down and jotted something on the map as Sliver spoke.

"It's a tricky business, this time spell. I've spent almost the entire time you've been gone digging through the archives. I haven't been able to find a way to lift it," Sliver said as Blake sighed in disappointment. "However," the dragon said holding up a finger, "I'm pretty sure I've figured out a way to link all the portals to our time here."

"Isn't that the same thing?" Blake asked.

"Not exactly. I'd still like to know how to undo the spell. All magic should be able to be undone." He scratched his chin. "And I don't like leaving a puzzle undone," he added, more to himself than to Blake.

"But it will work? And one day there won't be a year or more here?" Blake asked, leaning forward.

"I'm pretty certain. I've never done this particular spell before but I have practiced magic for quite a while. I'm no novice. But we won't know if I've been successful until you return."

"It'll work," Ajax said, patting Sliver on the shoulder. "Have more faith in yourself."

"I think the maps are ready," Neely said, setting down her pencil and nodding at her work. "We ought to have Niko and Leif look them over for accuracy in case I forgot anything."

Leif walked around the table and eyed the map. "When do we leave?" he asked as he scrutinized Neely's sketches. "And where are Sam and Niko?"

"We leave a couple hours before dusk," Ajax said. "We don't know what we'll be flying into. I'd like to travel by the cover of night, but the portal closes when the sun goes down, so we need to make sure we all get through before that happens. I don't think Striker will try to attack us when we come through, seeing as how he has a mission for us to complete, but he always does the unexpected, so it's better to be prepared."

"Niko and Sam are watching the portal just in case."

"So, what's the plan once we get there?" Blake asked.

Neely explained their idea to split up into two teams. Neely and Ajax would go to the Mer Realm, leaving Blake, Leif, and Sky to travel to the Animal Realm. Niko would enter with them but would then seek out Spots' family and deliver his remains. Sliver would fly them through the portal one at a time since they didn't know what to expect. Ajax would go first.

"Don't you think more of us should come?" Blake asked. "We're going into two worlds that we know nothing about. If something happens to one of us, we need others to carry on."

"We can't leave Rastella defenseless," Ajax explained.

"Sliver shall be here," Blake said. "He's the most powerful of all of us."

"But he can't be everywhere at once. Sliver and Ajax were both here when Striker came the first time and look what still happened," Neely said.

"I want to come too," Axel said as he moved into the main living area. Blake assumed he had been listening from the hallway.

"We've already been over this," Ajax said, sighing.

"I know," Axel said. "But I still *want* to accompany you. I don't want to be left behind to wonder if you're all right. I want to come but I won't. Neely and my brother are right, although it pains me to admit it." He winked at Ajax. "We need to have a constant watch on the portal when it's active. At least it closes at sunset. But during the daytime, one person alone can't shoulder that responsibility anymore. For years, one person was able to stand watch because the portal had never been used. But times have changed now. Just look at what happened. An entire elven army entered the portal. One person can't stand against that. And Rastella is still in shambles. Every able-bodied man still alive is attending the wounded and trying to rebuild. The king and queen can't spare anyone for the task. Some of us need to stay behind. Striker could send another army through for all we know. We have to leave a defense on this side."

"What about Squeak?" Blake asked. "He could come. Another cambriar that can change forms in a moment's notice might be helpful."

Sky bounded down from the kitchen counter; his cheeks stuffed with food. He tried to say something but no one could make it out. After a moment Sky swallowed the last remnants of food in his mouth.

"I doubt Squeak will ever leave his room again, let alone travel back through the portal with us," Sky said. "He's afraid of his own shadow."

Blake looked in the direction of Ajax's room where Squeak had taken up residency. "I'll talk to him. He assisted me once before. I think I can convince him to do it again."

Sky scoffed. "Good luck."

CHAPTER XII

Sky

Talk about a waste of time. There would be no convincing Squeak to join them on their mission fraught with danger. Being imprisoned and tortured had done a number on Sky's brother. Squeak might never be the same.

Dusk would be upon them before they knew it. Sky eyed the piles of supplies, everything in order, ready for their departure. Leif leaned over the kitchen table, adjusting the map. But Sky thought of one thing that only he could do.

Stacked on a small chair by the fireplace lay several large books. Sky asked Axel to bring them from the castle. He used his paw to turn the bright colored pages filled with images of animals and their environments.

As Sky scanned the pages, familiar animals met his gaze, some large and some small, but every few pages would be an animal unknown to him. Those he cataloged away in his mind in case he might need to shift forms.

"What are you looking at?" Ajax asked as he sat on the stone hearth of the fireplace.

"Animals. Just getting my arsenal ready. You never know what form might come in handy," Sky said, as he turned another page.

"Do you ever wonder when you'll find your true form?" Ajax asked, leaning forwards and peering down at the book.

Sky had asked himself this question a hundred times before. Once he locked into his true form he could never change again. Having the ability to shift species came in handy as he'd recently discovered with his brother. Squeak had changed into an animal Sky had never heard of to break Blake out of prison. Then he'd transformed into a dragon to fly the prince to safety and then later helped fly everyone through the portal to Rastella. And finally, he'd transformed into an armored mouse to escape the castle. The decision weighed heavily on Sky's mind. He did not want to make a mistake.

"It's something all cambriars think about. I've been in forms where my mind screamed for me to shift. Some forms are downright uncomfortable, others are just okay. But I don't wonder anymore."

Ajax raised a questioning eyebrow.

"This is it. A hoosula is the right form for me. I have no doubts. This just…well, it feels like me. I can't explain it."

Reaching forward, Ajax placed his hand on the book, preventing Sky from turning another page.

"Then why are you looking at these? What's the point?"

"Because they could help us save Niv. I can't lock into this shape until I know she's safe."

"But if this is your true shape, shouldn't you lock in? If you shift into another animal then you can never go back. You'll never be able to be a hoosula again."

"I know," Sky said, nodding as he pushed Ajax's hand off the book and resumed his search.

He'd do anything for Nivara. Getting her back home safely, that's all that mattered. Even if it meant he might be a little uncomfortable for the rest of his life.

"I don't know that anyone deserves a friend like you, but I suppose if anyone comes close it would be Niv," Ajax said.

"You were right," came a voice from across the room.

Sky didn't need to turn to know that Blake had returned from speaking with his brother.

"I'm not surprised," Sky said, not turning around. "He's been through a lot." Sky bit his tongue. The trauma came from Blake's father. If the king hadn't kept Squeak locked up in a tiny filthy cell for months, then he wouldn't be in his current state. Being imprisoned in Elf City had seemed like paradise compared to here.

"So, I guess it shall just be the five of us," Blake said, leaning against the wall and surveying the room. "Leif, Sky and me, and Ajax and Neely."

"I'm going to try to get some sleep while I still can," Ajax said, rubbing Sky's back as he rose. "I suggest the rest of you do the same." He let out a long yawn.

Sky turned as he heard the door open.

"Where do you think you're going?" Sky asked as Leif turned to head out.

"I need to say goodbye to Sam. I will be back before we need to leave."

"Give her my *love,"* Sky said, emphasizing the last word and grinning at Leif before his friend swung the door closed and left.

The others didn't wait long to take Ajax's advice. Neely curled up on the couch with a blanket, while Blake slunk into a chair and closed his eyes.

As much as Sky needed sleep, it would have to wait. Two more books needed to be scanned. He couldn't fire a bow, or swing a sword, or wave a magic finger at his enemies. His mind held his defenses, and Sky felt determined to fill it to the brim. He couldn't live with himself if he failed Nivara.

CHAPTER XIII

Ajax

"It's time," Ajax said, gently rousing Sky from the pile of books he'd fallen asleep on.

He turned next and woke Neely, who lay covered on the couch with one of his mother's heavy quilts.

She yawned but got up with haste, strapping on a cloak and then putting on her pack.

They all had cloaks, with the exception of Sky. Ajax found no hints to the climate of the other worlds. Cloaks could offer warmth and protection from the elements.

Axel loaned Blake his keeper's cloak. Since no magic ran in either of their veins it didn't help them to see magic. However, whether they could see it or not, dragon scales made up every keeper's cloak, making the cloak light, but also strong. It might offer Blake a little added protection should any fighting arise.

Unfortunately, Leif and Neely's cloaks were made from normal fabric. Edwin offered his cloak to Neely, but with magic just beginning to awaken in him, everyone thought it better if the cloak remained with him. Sliver could begin to train him which would be helpful if any elves came back through the portal.

The room felt odd. An unusual silence had fallen over the house. Unusual for the number of inhabitants that now resided in the home.

Unsurprisingly to Ajax, Blake waited by the door, the first ready to leave.

The young sorcerer carried a heavy weight on his shoulders. He had already lost one friend. It still felt surreal; he hadn't been given time to grieve. Ajax determined he would not lose another, even though at times he felt powerless—a sensation he hadn't experienced in quite some time. He'd have to find a way to save everyone.

They would be dividing and conquering from almost the moment they arrived. If something happened to Blake, Leif, Sky or Neely, he didn't know how he'd carry on. And Nivara…No, he couldn't let his mind go there. He needed to focus on what he could do and the things he knew for certain.

Ajax sat on the edge of the couch and pulled on his boots. He could hear his mother and father having a hushed discussion in the kitchen. He looked up to see Axel and his wife Sinda entering their main room as he fastened his keeper's cloak around his neck.

Leif handed Neely a map as Niko wrapped the jar of remains in a colored knit scarf to protect it before packing it in his own satchel.

"We should head out," Sliver said as he entered the cottage.

"Lead the way," Blake said, following him out.

Neely turned to Ajax's parents. "Thank you so much for your hospitality and kindness."

"Be safe," Mother Maxwell said as she embraced Neely goodbye. "Keep an eye on my son. I know he's got power but he's still a boy." She wiped her eyes with the sleeve of her shirt as she released the mermaid.

Ajax turned to Axel and gave him a giant bear hug. "Don't get complacent. Keep a keen watch on things. I want to come back to everything just as it is."

"I will. Between Sam, Sliver, and me…we will keep our home safe. Maybe father will even be doing magic by the time…" Axel began to tear up. "Just make sure you come back."

"What's everyone crying about?" Sky asked. "We shall be fine and we will return before you know it. You know we can't fail if I'm on the mission."

Axel laughed. "You're right of course, Sky. What were we thinking?"

Sky winked and sprung onto Niko's shoulder as the rhino strode outside. "Goodbye," he grunted.

Ajax gave his mother and father a quick embrace, or he tried to. His mother didn't want to release him.

"We're proud of you," Edwin called as Ajax and Neely stepped outside.

Ajax paused before closing the door. He should have said I love you, or thanks, or anything. But somehow that sounded like a goodbye, and Ajax just couldn't do it. Besides, his parents knew how he felt.

Once outside, Leif passed out the weapons in a quick and efficient manner. Armed and as prepared as they could be, they headed into the forest.

The portal loomed before them, swirling in menacing black waves. Ajax offered a silent prayer as Sliver approached the tree and chanted a spell in a language he did not understand. Sam stood a few feet back, armed with her bow, watching the portal for any unusual movement.

"Axel will be here in the morning to take the first shift," Leif whispered to Sam.

No one wanted to disturb Sliver, now in his dragon form. They all needed this spell to work.

The chanting fell silent and Sliver turned back to face the others.

"It is done," Sliver said.

"I suppose the time has come," Ajax said, stepping forward.

He had volunteered to be the first through the portal. With his magic and the dragon's, they would be the most equipped to handle any treachery planned by Striker.

Sliver knelt and lowered his wing, making it easier for Ajax to climb up onto the back of the big green dragon.

"I'll be back soon," Sliver said.

Ajax waved to his friends and turned back as Sliver flew into the portal.

As they emerged through the other side, Ajax's eyes widened in surprise. He didn't have to guess how Striker transported his elven army through the portal Ajax had placed miles down into an endless cavern. A platform had been constructed around the portal and attached to the side of the cavern. A staircase also ran up the cavern. Ajax couldn't see where it began. He couldn't even begin to guess how long it had taken Striker to construct it. Time acted differently here. Or it had. With any luck, Sliver's spell had taken care of that problem.

AJAX!

The voice boomed inside his head. Reflexively Ajax covered his ears with his hands, although he realized a moment later that it would do no good.

AJAX!

The voice boomed. Ajax groaned. The medallion must have been miles and miles from their location. He'd never heard it so loud. Ajax wondered if his eardrums could burst from the sound in his head. He tried to remember the spell that Sliver taught him to silence the amulet.

AJAX!

"Come on boy, remember what I taught you," Sliver said.

It was harder to concentrate than Ajax imagined, the voice pure agony in his head. But it would not get better until he silenced it. Ajax took a deep breath and said the words that Sliver taught him while picturing the amulet in his mind.

He cringed, waiting for the booming voice to come again, but it didn't.

"Well done," the dragon noted as he circled the platform. "What would you like me to do? Set you down here, or fly you up to the top?"

"I think it's better if we fly all the way up. It would take a long time to hike up all those stairs and we need to be sure there are not any surprises waiting for us."

"Hang on tight," Sliver said as he flapped his wings and soared upwards.

The wind whipped against Ajax with such force that he slipped, almost falling before he regained his balance.

"I told you to hang on," Sliver said.

"I'm trying," Ajax assured him as he tried to tighten his grip around the dragon's neck. "There's not much for me to grab hold of."

Other than the massive staircase, Ajax didn't see any sign of elves or evidence they had been here. Sliver deposited Ajax in the courtyard of the tower that had once been Axel's home, before diving back down to retrieve the others.

The time dragged on as Ajax waited for the others to arrive. While waiting, he checked the first few floors of the tower and found them empty and surprisingly clean—the beds made, cupboards stocked with food, and not a speck of dust lingered anywhere. Ajax chalked it up to magic and made a mental note to ask Sliver if he could teach him how to replicate it. It would be nice to never have to clean his house or worry about food.

Sometime later Blake and Neely arrived.

The prince dismounted first, assisting Neely off the dragon's back and onto the stone floor of the courtyard.

Sliver gave them a curt nod but wasted no more time before diving back into the cavern for his third and final trip.

Blake walked over to place his hands on the railing and looked down across the chasm.

Ajax joined him. "Sliver better hurry, or he'll be stuck here until tomorrow morning. The light is disappearing fast."

"At least nothing can get to the portal without our seeing it," Blake said.

They stood together in silence for a while before the prince spoke.

"It's so strange…being back here, I mean. It feels like a dream…and a nightmare. If that makes sense."

Ajax nodded. "I know. I never thought we'd be back here and under these circumstances. Who could have imagined this?"

"She's going to be okay though, right?"

Blake's eyes, red from worry and lack of sleep, looked at Ajax for reassurance, a desperate expression painting his face.

"Ye—" he began, but stopped suddenly.

Blake grabbed his arm. "What?"

"We're in the same world now. It might work," Ajax said, closing his eyes.

He assumed Blake understood since the prince did not disturb him.

Niv, are you there?

Ajax? Niv asked. *Is it really you?*

"She's alive," Blake sighed.

Ajax opened his eyes. He didn't have to explain it to Blake, he had read it from his expression.

CHAPTER XIV

Nivara

Telkin stepped back. "What do you think I'm going to do?" he asked, sounding shocked and appalled. He ran his hand down his long black braid and shook his head.

"Nothing," Niv said, sticking her chin out in defiance. "You're not going to lay a finger on me."

"I have no intention of touching you. I helped you, and now you are going to return the favor."

"What could I possibly assist you with?" Niv asked, confused. Locked in a prison cell, what help could she be? Maybe he just wanted her to let her guard down. Niv wouldn't fall for it.

"I want answers. I want to know everything there is to know about Leif."

She wondered what he could want to know about Leif. Striker would know all about his son. Telkin couldn't expect that Nivara would aid him in capturing Leif.

"I won't help you hurt him. Do what you want to me, but I won't tell you anything that you can use against him," Niv said, stepping back until her back pressed against the cold stone wall. She glanced around the small cell looking for a weapon. A small stool sat a few feet away but Telkin stood by it. If it had been closer, she could have picked it up and hit him over the head with it.

"I don't want to hurt him, I just want to know what he's like," Telkin said, sounding curious. He reached for the small stool and pulled it closer to him.

For a moment, Niv thought that maybe he'd had the same idea as she and planned to beat the answers out of her. But he had access to any weapon he wanted.

Telkin set the stool down and took a seat.

"But why?" Niv pressed.

"Leif is my brother."

CHAPTER XV

Sky

The sun had almost set by the time Sliver made his final appearance. Leif, Niko, and Sky climbed up onto the dragon's back.

"I may not be back tonight," Sliver said, craning his neck around to where Sam waited.

"You won't," she said. "Not if how long you've been gone on your previous trips is any indication."

"With any luck Axel won't try to shoot me when I come through in the morning," Sliver said.

"If he did, it would just bounce off your scales," Sky noted. "What's there to be worried about? I, on the other hand, could miss dinner if we don't get moving."

"We wouldn't want that," Niko said.

"No, we would not," Leif agreed. "You have no idea how grumpy this one gets when he has missed a meal." Leif laughed, rubbing Sky on his back as the dragon took flight.

If not for the back rub, Sky might have taken offense to the comment. But he let it go. He loved a good back rub.

The sun dipped behind the horizon moments after Sliver flew through the portal.

Cutting it a little close, Sky thought.

The light faded into gray and then black as Sliver flew upward. Sky felt grateful for the ride. The long staircase would not have been fun to ascend. The workmanship looked a little shoddy and unstable too. He hoped it held up for the trip home.

Home.

When had he started thinking of Rastella as home? He couldn't pinpoint a moment. But it did feel like home.

An aroma of some type of roasted fowl flowed into his nostrils. Sky's ears perked up, and he looked up to see them nearing the top of the cavern at last.

His stomach growled as Sliver landed in the courtyard where a cooking fire burned with Neely turning several birds on a skewer.

Ajax opened a door from inside the tower and stepped out, holding a tray laden with fruit, cheeses, and bread.

"You're just in time," Ajax said with a smile. "This will be the best meal we have."

He popped a grape in his mouth and set the tray on a blanket near the fire.

Blake followed behind him with some glasses and a pitcher filled with purple liquid. He looked a little more at ease. Maybe the fact that they arrived here at last had helped release some of Blake's tension.

"I'm famished," Sky said, bounding off the dragon's back.

"Really?" Ajax asked sarcastically.

Sliver reverted to his human form and they all settled down on the stone floor to eat.

Blake explained to the others how Ajax had been able to reestablish his mental connection to Nivara. Striker locked her in a dungeon buried far beneath the surface, but Niv was alive and had not been harmed yet.

When the last of the cheese and bread had been eaten, Blake rose. He brushed the dust off the back his trousers and cleared his throat.

"I just want to offer my gratitude to each of you," he said. "Thank you for coming here to help me free Nivara."

"We all care for her," Neely said. "We can't just abandon her to Striker. She would never give up on us."

"I know, and I know she loves each of you," Blake said. "But I still offer my thanks."

"We should get some rest. Tomorrow we split up, find our ingredients, and if everything goes well, meet back here in a day or two," Ajax said. Then he turned to Niko. "Please give Spots' family my condolences. He died a hero. Let them know I owe Spots a debt. If there is ever anything I can do, if it's within my power I will."

Niko placed his large hoof on Ajax's shoulder. "I will. I wish I could be in two places at once. But I owe this to Spots. His family needs to spread his ashes. If they are not laid to rest soon, Spots will never know peace on the other side."

"We all understand," Ajax said. "After everything he did for us, none of us wants to dishonor his memory by not carrying out his family's wishes."

Sky wished Niko could go with them. His skill with an ax could not be matched. His bulky size alone would keep many from wanting to attack them. Sky didn't think it mattered when the ladybug's ashes got spread throughout the land. Spots died a hero; how could he not find peace? He didn't think another few days would make a difference, but Niko thought so.

Unsure of when he'd get another hot meal, Sky finished off the last scraps of the roasted birds. He couldn't stand seeing anything go to waste and the rest of the journey he'd be stuck with nothing more than dried meat.

Sleep evaded Sky, his thoughts focused on Nivara. He thought hearing the news that she lived would help him sleep easier. But Sky had lived in that castle for a long time. He knew what kind of elf Striker was: a master manipulator, torturer, and general psychopath. Being alive didn't mean being safe.

Sky must have fallen asleep at some point because Blake shook him gently awake in the morning.

"It's time to go. We'll eat on the road. We need to get across before the bridge disappears," Blake said. Then he reached for his satchel and secured his bedroll.

Sky stretched, arching his back until it popped. "Okay, let's go."

A quiet bustle surrounded him. Ajax reached back over his shoulder and counted the arrows in his quiver, nodding to himself before sliding his bow over his shoulder.

Neely stood ready to go, her pack on. She helped Leif secure his bedroll as he tested the sharpness of his daggers with the tip of his finger.

Sky looked around but didn't see the dragon. He must have already flown back to Rastella. His eyes searched for Niko but he too had gone.

"Are you ready, Leif?" Blake asked.

"Ready." Leif trotted over and knelt, allowing Sky to scurry up his shoulder.

"I guess this is goodbye for now," Sky said, his gaze meeting Ajax's, and then Neely's. "Be safe."

"You too," Neely said, tears welling up her in eyes.

"See you soon," Ajax said, clasping Leif's arm, and giving a farewell nod to the prince.

Both groups hurried onto the almost transparent bridge. Sky felt a pang in his heart. Last time he stood here, Niv had been with them. Would he ever see her again?

They waved farewell and each group headed in a different direction. Ajax and Neely to the east to find the portal to the Mer Realm, and Blake, Leif, and Sky to the west to find the portal to the Animal Realm.

CHAPTER XVI

Ajax

Neely's graceful strides could not be overlooked. Even with his best friend locked away in a dungeon, it surprised Ajax that he could still see beauty in the world.

Neely ran ahead of Ajax. There should still be time, but neither of them wanted to be stuck on a magical bridge over an endless chasm when it disappeared so they decided to err on the side of caution.

Ajax lumbered after Neely. His legs, being shorter than hers, made him have to work harder to keep up the pace that appeared effortless to Neely.

Once across the chasm and with solid earth beneath his feet, Ajax collapsed, panting. Why didn't Neely look out of breath?

With effort Ajax pushed himself to his feet and tried to calm his breathing. A dark forest towered before them. He had never entered the forest of Never Ending Night, he had only heard about it from Blake and Sliver.

Blake had flown through it, a forest so dark that Ajax wouldn't even be able to make out his hand in front of his face. Yet somewhere in the vast darkness before them lay the portal to the Mer Realm. A portal thought lost forever. And in truth, maybe it was. What if Ajax couldn't find it?

Sliver had been trying to teach Ajax how to sense magic, but the lessons had been rushed. Between searching for answers about the other worlds and the invincibility elixir and finding a way to fix the spell that altered time on the portal, their hands had been full.

No torch would burn, nor fire would light, inside the forest. It seemed impossible although Ajax didn't doubt Sliver's words. He'd seen plenty of impossible in the last year or two.

Only one source of light could penetrate the darkness of the forest. A small glowing rock called a star stone. Although they didn't have one of these stones, Sliver had been able to spell a stone to mimic the same glow, but it wouldn't last forever. Using the light came at a steep price.

Vampire bats.

Well, that's what Ajax called them because he couldn't pronounce the name that Sliver had used. But that's what they were. Sliver described them as furry black monsters attracted to light. They slept all day in hidden caves beneath the forest, but the light called to them like nothing else. These beasts would burrow up from the ground and latch onto anything that moved, sinking their razor-sharp fangs into them, and draining them of every last drop of blood.

Hence vampire bats.

Ajax wondered if these bat-like creatures had any influence like the fictional vampires that existed in storybooks back home.

"So, we're both agreed?" Ajax asked, hoping Neely might have come up with a better plan. "We go in blind. I try to sense the magic and if I do, we use the light fast to find the portal and enter it."

"Agreed," Neely said, stretching her hand out towards him. "So we don't lose each other."

He reached forward and gripped her hand. "Here we go."

Before he could take a step forward Ajax heard a noise above his head. He looked upward and saw a pair of langabeasts ridden by two elven soldiers descending towards them.

Before they could land, Ajax had his bow aimed at one and Neely had a long spear pointed towards the second elf.

"We bring a message from Lord Striker," the elf Ajax targeted said. "He is tired of waiting; in two days he shall execute his prisoner."

"Two days!" Ajax exclaimed. "That's not enough time. We have to go to two different realms."

"Not our problem." the elf shrugged, pulling back on his animal's reigns, trying to keep him grounded. "We have no power to negotiate. We came to deliver a message, nothing more. But it's about time you finally got here. We've been checking every day for your arrival, and now we can go home."

Before Ajax could think of anything else to say, they kicked their langabeasts in the flanks and flew off towards the south.

"Two days," Ajax muttered in disbelief.

"We don't have any time to lose," Neely said, grabbing Ajax by the hand and pulling him into the forest.

Within a couple of steps, darkness encompassed them. It felt eerie. Ajax had never been in anything like it. At home, even on the darkest night, the stars and the moon offered some light. The darkness disoriented him. He peered over his shoulder, thinking he should at least be able to see some light from where they just entered, but saw nothing.

"We'll have to try walking with one foot straight in front of the other to ensure we are heading deeper into the woods and not backtracking," Ajax said in a whisper.

A shiver ran down his spine. He couldn't hear anything, not a bird nor the wind. The unnatural silence unnerved him.

They made their way through the trees at a slow and steady pace. Ajax felt roots and rocks beneath his boots and worried that if they fell it might turn them around and they'd lose any sense of direction they maintained.

At least they didn't have to worry about anything attacking them in here. Other than the vampire bats, no other life lived in this forest. What would want to live like this?

As they continued deeper into the forest, or at least they hoped they continued to head further in, Ajax would squeeze Neely's hand to make sure she was still there. Sometimes he would feel her doing the same. They lost almost all their senses in here, consumed by the darkness.

Ajax closed his eyes out of habit from his mental exercises

and tried to sense any source of magic, but felt none. He tried off and on for what felt like hours, although he had no way of knowing how much time had passed.

"How do you think the others are faring?" Ajax whispered. For some reason he felt like he needed to be quiet. In the blackness he couldn't help but remember all the scary stories Axel used to tell him growing up.

"Better than us," Neely said in hushed tones. "I'm beginning to wish I'd gone with them. We could get lost in here forever. I don't think we thought out our plan very well."

"If only I had my medallion. It might help me sense the magic better. Plus, it would have repelled the bats and we could have used the light more."

They continued their slow-paced drudging through the woods. Ajax's boots, now wet from a small creek they traversed, made his journey more uncomfortable. Or at least, he hoped it had been a creek.. His mind conjured up images of ghosts and streams filled with blood. Anything could be in here and they'd have no idea.

Panic consumed him until he couldn't contain it anymore. He yelled, partly in frustration and partly in fear that they'd never leave this place.

"I was about to do the same thing." Neely laughed. "Does it make you feel better?"

"As a matter of fact, it did. My head feels a little clearer."

Neely let out a scream.

"That does feel better. I guess we don't need to whisper anymore."

They continued moving blindly through the forest when Neely pulled on Ajax's hand.

"Let's see if we can find a place to sit and eat something. I'm getting hungry."

Ajax took another step forward then stopped. Neely moved passed him but he pulled her back.

"Believe it or not, I think I'm feeling a trickle of magic."

"Oh thank goodness," Neely said, relief evident in her voice. "We can eat later."

"Now let's pray I can follow it."

With each step forward Ajax's confidence grew. The trickle of magic became bigger. Soon he could feel a pulsing.

"I think this is it," Ajax said.

"Okay."

"Remember, we need to be quick. According to Sliver these vampire bats are wicked fast. So we look for the portal and once we see it, we jump. Don't wait for me. Any second we waste could be deadly."

"We ought to arm ourselves just in case," Neely suggested.

Ajax and Neely released their hands. It felt so wrong after being each other's lifeline in this abysmal place. He reached for his sword and pulled it with care from its sheath, not wanting to bump his friend with it.

He could hear her shift and imagined her holding her spear,

ready to strike.

"Ready?" he asked.

"To be able to see something, anything? You bet."

Ajax reached into his satchel and felt for the rough stone. "Here goes," he told her as he pulled it up and held it forward in front of them.

Their eyes scanned the area frantically.

"Over there," Neely shouted as she pointed to a large swirling vortex hovering a few hundred feet in front of them.

"Run!" Ajax yelled, holding the light up with one hand while gripping his sword tightly with the other.

He hadn't brought them close enough. He thought they'd be a few feet away. The ground rumbled beneath them as dirt sprayed up all around them.

"Keep going," Ajax yelled.

The portal stood a hundred feet away when the first creature emerged. It darted forward lightning quick, but Ajax slashed his sword with as much force as he could muster, sending the bat flying backwards screeching and falling.

Ajax risked a glance over his shoulder and saw a dozen more emerging. They weren't as big as Ajax imagined but their eyes glowed with a ferocity that sent chills down his spine.

Soon a blur of furry monsters swarmed them. Neely jabbed with her spear, staking one and then throwing it into another. Ajax swung his sword like a maniac. Too many bats emerged, making it hard to see where to attack. He felt something sharp sink into his shoulder but continued to push forward. He waved the hand holding the light behind them, sending a magic tidal wave of air at them. It knocked the majority back in a tumultuous tumble. But with so many bats emerging, a majority was still not enough.

Looking forward Ajax could see the bats closing in on the portal. Neely ran in front a mere few feet from the portal. Two bat creatures clung to her, one on her thigh and another on her back, but she fought forward, lunging her sharp spear at the ones that swarmed her.

Neely reached the portal but paused to look back.

"Go!" Ajax yelled.

She leapt forward and the bats released her, fleeting away from the portal.

Another set of sharp fangs dug into Ajax's leg. He could feel stabbing all over him. He'd lost count of how many of these blood-sucking leeches had attached themselves to him. He felt faint and weak. The more they latched on to him the harder Ajax had to push to move forward.

He felt so tired. He waved his hand, sending a few of the oncoming bats back, but it did nothing for the ones already on him.

Slowly the pain faded and he felt sleep on the verge of overtaking him. But Niv's image floated into his mind—Lord Striker standing over her, stabbing her as he had in the courtyard of Axel's tower. A burst of adrenaline shot through him. He didn't care what happened to him, but he wouldn't let Nivara die. He had to make it to the portal. Ajax ran forward in an awkward sprint and fell into the portal.

CHAPTER XVII

Blake

The bridge shimmered beneath Blake's feet, revealing a cavern that many thought never ended. Blake, thankfully, had never been afraid of heights. He strode forward, following Leif and Sky. They knew this land, and even with the map, Blake felt better letting someone who lived here take charge…for now.

He peered over his shoulder to glance at his friends one last time and noticed Ajax and Neely in a sprint.

"Are you certain that we have sufficient time to cross this?" Blake asked, feeling a little weary for the first time since stepping foot on this near-invisible bridge.

"Yes, we should have time," Leif said.

"But Ajax and Neely are running?"

"They're just eager," Sky said, although Blake noticed some hesitance in his voice.

"I am sure we are fine," Leif said. "But we are in a hurry, so perhaps it might be prudent for us to run also."

Leif and Sky darted forward before Blake had a chance to respond. He ran after them, panting as they collapsed on the ground on the other side of the cavern.

Blake and Leif watched the sky bridge, but it didn't dissolve like they imagined.

"Well, I guess you were right, Sky. They were just eager." Blake laughed, a little embarrassed.

"I think it startled us all," Leif said. "But we'd better get going. It is quite a trek to the Stinking Bogs."

"Do you think you'll find your mother there?" Blake asked.

"No," Leif said, pausing for a moment before adding, "I mean, Striker brings back new elves yearly. I don't know how any of us would be able to tell who our mother is. Or how they'd be able to tell us apart. We're quite young when he brings us back." A look of despair shadowed his face and Blake wished he could take back his question.

"I'm so sorry," Blake said as he pulled his cowl up over his head. Despite the earliness of the hour, the heat beat down on them in a relentless fashion.

"It's fine," Leif said. "I've lived my entire life without a mother. But I am curious to meet the female elves. See what they are like. Find out what lies Striker told them to keep them away from us."

"I do find it difficult to fathom how any mothers can just hand off their children, never to see them again," Blake said. "But knowing Striker, this is just another of his twisted games."

Sky looked anywhere but at the two of them, probably not wanting to get anywhere near this conversation.

They skirted the edge of the Slumbering Forest. Cutting through the forest was the direct route, but I came with one perilous obstacle: plants that could put anyone who came into their vicinity to sleep, indefinitely. Not wanting to take the risk and not having a sorcerer with them to conjure up a magical preventative made the longer route more appealing.

After a couple of hours of brisk walking, Blake smelled something awful.

"I take it we're getting closer?" he asked, pinching the bridge of his nose with his fingers.

"I think so. No one ever ventures too close, so I'm not sure."

The stench made Blake's eyes water. He tried breathing through his mouth and then his nose, but nothing lessened the intensity of the odor.

"I think Ajax and Neely got the better end of this deal," Sky said, gagging. "Are there any animals in your world that can't smell? Because I'd consider changing into anything at the moment if it got rid of this aroma."

"Me too," Blake agreed.

"Well, be glad you're human. My senses are more heightened. So as bad as it smells to you, it's worse for me," Sky said.

Blake shuddered. "I can't imagine how it could be any worse. You have my condolences, Sky."

They made their way towards the smell. Soon water spread out in front of them as far as the eye could see. Bright turquoise moss littered the surface of the bog.

"Sky, want to shift into your bigger size and carry us through this mess?" Blake asked.

"Not on your life. I hate being wet. Wet and smelling are even worse. I'll stay right here," he said, nuzzling up to Leif's neck.

Blake turned to examine the bright moss. "Oh my," he choked. "I think the moss is what's causing the stench.

"Avoid the moss. Good to know," Leif said, using his sword to push the moss out of his way.

Leif moved forward, sloshing through the bog. Blake watched for a moment and then resigned himself to follow.

For Nivara, he thought.

The water deepened as they made their way north. First the water reached his mid-calf but as they continued it rose until it reached his waist. They carried their packs above their heads to keep them dry.

All of a sudden, Leif took a step and disappeared.

"Leif!" Blake called.

The elf's head resurfaced, and he sputtered water from his mouth. "Sky?"

Sky reappeared a moment later.

"So much for staying dry," he muttered as he dog paddled back over to Leif. "And in case you were wondering, the water tastes horrible." He spit into the lake. "Ugh!"

"It is slippery here and there's quite a drop-off. I was not expecting it." Leif had regained his footing and the water now rose to his shoulders. Sky climbed back on, staying partially submerged.

The elf took out his waterskin and rinsed his mouth out, then offered some to Sky who did the same.

"What would you think if I shrank into my smallest size and rode on your head?" Sky asked.

"I think you can be miserable like the rest of us," Leif said.

"Trust me, I'd still be miserable," Sky muttered as he rearranged himself on Leif's shoulder, holding his tail up out of the bog.

Blake laughed and then cringed as he stepped down the drop-off with Leif's assistance, holding his bundle above his head with his other hand.

The icy water chilled him to the bone. Blake hoped that he would get used to it soon. At least his pack remained dry. A bonus for letting the elf take the lead.

They hadn't taken more than a few steps when Leif disappeared in front of him for a second time.

Great, another drop-off, Blake thought. He waited for his friend to reappear.

Sky emerged first, sputtering and coughing. He climbed onto Blake's shoulder.

"I'm getting sick of this bog," Sky said as he shivered from the cold. "I think I'll stick with you for a while."

They looked around, waiting for Leif to resurface.

"Leif?" Blake asked, growing more concerned as the seconds passed by. Why hadn't he resurfaced yet?

"Leif!" Sky yelled.

About twenty feet from where they stood, Leif punched through the surface of the water, gasping for air. A thick hairy black claw clutched his body.

Blake dove forward, dropping his bag and flinging Sky to the side in the process.

As he swam towards Leif, three pulsing green eyes rose out of the water. Leif struggled trying to get his hands free, but the claw held him in place.

When Blake reached Leif he drew his sword, thankful that the water level dropped here. He swung his sword at the creature, hacking off a second claw that shot towards him. Losing a limb didn't faze the creature.

Blake continued to swing left and right, hacking at any part of the monster he could see. The eyes dodged around, making Blake wish he had Leif's bow. The elf must have dropped it.

"Sky, Leif's bow!" Blake called as he continued to hack off claw after claw.

How many claws can this thing have? Blake wondered.

The water opened up, swirling into a giant whirlpool. Blake dug his feet into the mud as the current pulled him toward it. Inside he could see a mouth opening with a long-toothed tentacle-like tongue that sped straight for him.

Blake dove under the water just as it whipped above his head. When he resurfaced, Blake noticed Leif being dragged towards the mouth.

The tongue struck towards Blake a second time and he deflected it with his sword.

"Prince Blake," Sky called.

The prince turned and found Sky in his bigger size paddling towards him, clinging to the bow with one paw and arrows with his other paw.

"Hurry," Blake shouted as he swung his sword at the tongue again. A bright red gash opened on his shoulder as his swing failed to deflect the entire blow. Blake winced as pain blossomed across the area.

Blake looked on in horror as Leif now dangled almost directly over the creature's mouth.

"Here," Sky said, pushing the bow into Blake's hand.

The prince dropped his sword and grimaced as he nocked an arrow and aimed it at the creature's mouth. He groaned as he released it. The arrow flew straight into the mouth.

They waited in anticipation, but nothing happened.

Blake looked down at the two remaining arrows.

"Go for the eyes," Sky said.

The lidless glowing eyes wove in and out around Leif's body.

"Hurry!" Sky urged.

He'd always been a fine shot, but not as amazing as Leif. Blake prayed he'd have some luck on his side.

He sucked in his breath, nocked another arrow, and let it fly at the closest eye.

It struck true. Dead center. The creature wailed and thrashed.

"Hurry, shoot another one."

Blake fired his last arrow and breathed a sigh of relief. Luck had not deserted him. The second arrow struck another eye.

The monster dropped Leif, who hung straight above the swirling mouth. But before the elf could hit the water, the creature disappeared below the surface, shrieking in agony.

Leif resurfaced, pulling a dagger from his waist, spinning around in a panic, waiting for the creature to attack again.

"I think it's gone," Blake said after a minute. "Are you okay?"

Leif nodded. "I think I shall be black and blue by tonight, but I shall live. The claws put pressure on my torso, but they had no sharpness to them." His eyes widened and he pointed to Blake's shoulder. "How are you? That cut looks deep. I think it will need to be sewed up."

"I'll live," Blake said. "We need to find our gear and get out of here. My bag had the dragon eggshells in it." He hit himself in the head with the palm of his hand and then shook his head. "I'm so stupid. I never should have kept them all. The shells ought to have been divided between us in case anything happened."

His heart began to beat faster as panic consumed him. What would he do if he lost the dragon eggshells? They had not time to return and get more. Blake took a deep breath. He needed to remain calm. They had to find them.

"We can worry about that later," Sky said. "I, for one, do not want to encounter another one of those monsters. Who's to say there aren't more? Or that the one we fought won't lick its wounds and return to try to finish what it started. Let's find our stuff and get out of here."

Blake dove under the murky water time and time again. He tried opening his eyes, but could see nothing. He ran his hands along the bottom of the marsh feeling mud and rocks.

"I found my quivers!" Leif shouted, elated at the discovery.

Sky and Blake began searching in the same vicinity.

He'd almost given up hope when Blake's finger brushed across fabric. He grabbed hold of it, offering a silent prayer that he'd found his own bag rather than the elf's. Holding his breath, he pulled the heavy bag out of the water.

It was his.

Unfortunately they lost the elf's pack and both their bedrolls but they didn't want to delay any longer

At least we recovered the dragon shells, Blake thought, feeling a huge weight lift off him. They could survive without the rest.

They trudged through the bog in silence for a while, stepping with care and listening for the sound of any approaching monsters.

Then Sky broke the silence.

"Hey, look. I'm out of the water." He shook his fur and then stopped when he noticed Leif's glare. "Sorry, I didn't mean to get you wet."

Leif wiped his face with his hand.

They continued on for another few minutes.

"I think Sky's right. It is getting shallower," Blake noted.

"And inclining," Leif said. "Look, there's dry land up ahead."

"What's past the Stinking Bogs?" Blake asked.

"Nothing." Leif shrugged. "I mean, no one knows. We never come here."

Blake stopped—he could have sworn he just heard laughter.

Leif must have heard it too because he turned back and smiled. "It looks like we might have found the elf mothers."

CHAPTER XVIII

Nivara

"Brother? Leif doesn't have a brother," Niv said, wondering where the elf thought he could get with this lie. Leif didn't talk about his childhood often. He didn't have many fond memories. But Niv knew for a fact that his family consisted of him and Striker. And if he admitted to having a deranged elf as a father, why hold back any more of the family tree?

"He has two sisters as well, but he is unaware of the fact. I don't understand why Father never told him about us," Telkin said, rubbing his chin. "A lot about Father is confusing."

He knew how to act, Niv had to give him that. Telkin looked confused.

"You'll have to do better than that if you want to convince me," Niv said. "If you're his brother, where have you been all this time and how could he not know?"

"I've lived with my mother for most of my life. Elves have many traditions. Father found a safe refuge for his people out past the Stinking Bogs after the attack on our city. It's beautiful. It's surrounded by a deadly bog that keeps us safe. None of the creatures from the realms have tried to attack us there. They are too afraid of what lurks beneath the surface."

"Safe from what?" Niv asked. "The only threat to the realms

is the elves."

"Lies fall so easily from your lips. We are safe from the rest of the realms. Before I was born, the elves lived somewhere else. A paradise. We lived there in peace, but sorcerers, and the merpeople, turned on us. They wanted to conquer the realms. They hunted my kind down, trying to exterminate us. Father found this haven for us to hide in, while he and the elven armies have been fighting for years trying to reclaim our homeland."

How did Lord Striker brainwash all of the elves into believing this? Niv wondered.

"That still doesn't answer why Leif is here and you were there?"

Telkin nodded. "As elves we all have a responsibility to our people. Dark-haired elves are given the task of protecting the women and children, while the elves born with white hair are bound to the army. Father always believed that white-haired elves were more apt at fighting, but he returned a few months ago and said he wanted to give some of us the opportunity to try our hand at battle. He said if we had a larger army, we could take back our homeland sooner and all be reunited.

"But I don't understand how any elf could betray his family. That's why I want to know about Leif. I suppose that's why Father let us believe he'd died. To spare mother of knowing the pain of having a son like him. Father sensed the darkness in him even as a child."

Niv had no idea how to answer Telkin. Like Leif, he had been lied to his entire life. Leif had been raised with cruelty and saw past some of his father's lies, but even he had found it hard to believe that elf mothers existed after being lied to his entire life. How would Telkin react to the truth? Would he believe Nivara over his own blood?

"I don't know that I can give you the answer to that question," Niv said. "But I'll tell you how I met your brother."

She proceeded to give him an account of how she came to be in his world. How Leif and Sky were the first inhabitants she met and how they dropped everything to aid her, risking their lives for her and saving her more than once.

"Why would he assist you? Did you promise him power? Did you offer to help to overthrow my father? There must be some reason."

"He is kind. Leif saw someone in need and helped them, simple as that."

"I fear you are full of lies and deceit like him," Telkin said, standing up. "I'm wasting my time. My father is trying to save the elves. He's been good to me." Telkin pointed to his uniform, his black tunic with a red sash adorning it. "He's seen my skill, made me a captain, and trusted me with the most important tasks. Everything he does is for his people."

"You call me a liar. But even you admitted that Striker already lied to you. A truth he's hidden not only from you but from your mother as well. You said you lived with the elf mothers and children. Have you ever seen an evil baby? Does your father radiate kindness? I think you just want to believe the worst. Then you won't have to face the truth of who your father is. It took Leif years to accept that Striker wouldn't change and find the courage to leave him. I guess I can't expect you to realize it in a day."

Niv thought she saw a flash of uncertainty on his face as he turned and banged hard on the door.

"If you want to know more, you know where to find me," Niv said.

They waited in silence as a whistle summoned the troll. Telkin gave Nivara a second glance as the cell door opened and he stormed out.

Maybe she had said too much. Pushed too much on him at once. She thought of how Leif dreamed of meeting his mother and he'd only become aware of her existence in the last few days. What must it be like for Telkin, to have known about his father his entire life? Seen him leave year after year taking other elves that he felt had more potential. Then at last coming and giving Telkin the chance to prove himself to the savior of the elves, Lord Striker. Even if she could break through to him, to destroy this fantasy vision he had of his father, she had no time.

From all Nivara heard, Striker had not mastered the art of being patient. He would not leave her here long. And when he did summon her...she couldn't let her mind go there.

CHAPTER XIX

Ajax

Ajax opened his eyes, finding himself lying on a sandy beach. Every inch of his body ached. Neely lay sprawled out a few feet away, breathing heavily. Little more than rags remained of her cloak, and Ajax hoped it had offered some protection.

The dragon scales that made up his cloak made it impenetrable, but the vampire bats just got underneath it as he ran. It may have delayed them for a moment, but since Ajax ran behind Neely more of the bats converged on him.

But he preferred that. He wished he could have saved Neely from some of this.

Naught could have made Ajax move. He felt more exhausted than he had felt in his entire life. He wanted to call out to Neely and ask her how she felt but he couldn't force his lips to move. Just keeping his eyes open took so much effort.

Ajax had no idea how much time passed before Neely sat up. She turned towards him and called out.

"Are you all right?" she asked as she rose to her feet, looking unsteady. "You received the brunt of the attack."

"I'll be fine," Ajax croaked.

Dried blood covered Neely's shoulder, but at least she

wasn't bleeding anymore. She limped towards him and knelt beside him.

"Do you think you can walk?" Neely asked, leaning forward and inspecting his various injuries.

Ajax could see the concern on her face.

"I think," Neely continued, "if we can find my people... well, they must have medicine or healers...some kind of help."

"I'll try. I got the brunt of the attack from the bats, but I also have magic in my blood. It helps me heal. I think without it I would be dead." Ajax said.

He reached forward and grasped Neely's hand as she pulled him up into a sitting position. Ajax felt a wave of dizziness come over him. After a few moments it passed and Neely helped him to his feet. He swayed, but Neely steadied him, using her uninjured leg to plant them both up firmly.

Having been flat on his back since they arrived, Ajax hadn't gotten a good look at this new world. A few hundred feet down the beach, he saw the ruins of what must have been the city where the elves had lived at one time. Little more than crumbled rubble remained. If Ajax hadn't known a city used to be here, he never would have known that's what the broken bits of stone had once been. Time erased almost all the evidence of its existence.

"I would imagine quite a bit has changed in the last few hundred years. But Sliver said that in the city there used to be a way for elves and other creatures to come down to the city of the merpeople." He shrugged. "I guess that's where we should start searching first. I can't believe I will be going to a city built underwater. It seems so impossible to me. I wonder what they engineered to transport those of us without gills down there."

The walk felt like miles. Ajax could imagine how pathetic they looked lumbering down the beach. The sand made it difficult to walk. The image of Nivara being locked in a damp cell somewhere, frightened and cold, kept him going.

By the time they stopped to rest on a large rock, sweat covered Ajax.

"You are so lucky," he said.

"Why?" Neely asked, perplexed.

"You don't sweat. I hate wearing wet clothes," Ajax said, wringing out the bottom of his shirt.

She shrugged. "Even if I did, I don't dislike being wet as much as you." She grinned wryly. "Maybe I should just go down and swim about. I could find another mermaid and find out how to get you down to the city."

"I don't like the idea of us separating," he said. "At least not yet. What if all the merpeople aren't good?"

Neely looked appalled at his comment.

"I mean, not all humans are good…" she still looked upset, so he continued. "Just look what happened with Blake's father. Maybe I'm not saying this right. I just think sometimes there can be misunderstandings, and it might be better for us to stay together. Let's search for a while more."

"All right," she said, looking a little appeased.

They continued trudging through the sand until Ajax couldn't stand the heat anymore.

"It's too hot. I need to splash some water on my face," Ajax said.

Neely helped him to the water's edge, careful not to get too wet. The tops of her feet had already become scaly, just from the little bit of water that had splashed across them.

Ajax bent down and relished the feeling of the chilly water hitting his knees. He scooped up a handful of the refreshing liquid and dumped it over his head. Some dripped in his mouth. It didn't taste salty.

With this new revelation, Ajax cupped his hands and filled them with more water, then drizzled it in his mouth. The cold and refreshing liquid tasted better than the warm water in his waterskin.

He reached his hands in a second time and noticed something mossy just beneath the surface. The rest of the water looked crystal clear. He reached down and felt something hard and cold underneath the slimy moss.

More curious than anything, Ajax dug around it determined to uncover its secret.

"Neely, look at this."

As he continued to dig, Ajax unearthed links forming a long chain with a harness attachment buried beneath the surface.

"I think that's what we're looking for," Neely said, as she

knelt in the dry sand and started digging.

It took a while but the chain led them to a large clear globe. Once all the sand had been dug up from around the ball, it stood as high as Ajax's chin. Inside, secured to the bottom of the globe, sat a lone chair with straps. Above the chair hung bright colored plant life.

"I guess that's where I go?" Ajax said, not feeling super confident. "I hope it's still airtight after all this time."

Together they inspected the ball and didn't see any cracks or openings besides a small door. The chain, although covered in moss, still felt solid.

"You get inside and secure yourself. I'll go and put on the harness," Neely said, sounding much more enthused than Ajax felt.

"Are you sure you can pull me with your injuries?" Ajax asked.

"I'll be fine. Swimming is a lot easier than walking and my body yearns to shift and be back under water. Plus, as I get larger these injuries will get smaller, so they won't bother me that much."

"Okay," Ajax said as he pried the door open and climbed inside.

He used the straps to secure himself as best as he could, then waited. He felt a small tug, and before he could prepare himself, the globe shot forward.

Ajax gripped the sides of the chair, holding on for dear life.

He plunged down into the water, a massive creature swimming in front of him. The globe swirled upside down for a moment but as Neely's pace evened out the globe righted itself.

Ajax forgot how big Neely became when she transformed, like a large shark-like creature.

The sea blurred by as the mermaid sped through the water. Neely had told him the truth—her injuries didn't seem to be bothering her now that she'd transformed. Ajax saw bright colorful fish and glowing plant life. He wondered if any of them could be the mystical glow flower they had come to collect.

As they continued deeper into the water another thought occurred to Ajax. He'd been so preoccupied about making sure water couldn't get into the container that he hadn't thought about how air got in.

He started to panic, looking around for any sign of a city. Ajax was about to open his mind up to Neely and have her surface when he realized they had been submerged for quiet a while. He slowed his breathing and took in large deliberate breaths. It didn't feel difficult. There still seemed to be plenty of air. He examined the structure carrying him, it must contain some type of magical properties. Besides he was not the first to travel this way to the mermaid city. He just needed a little faith.

Ajax lost track of time as Neely dragged him through the water. Without the sun to guide him, he had no idea the hour.

All of a sudden, a silver creature sped over his head. Then it whipped around and shot towards Neely.

The fish-like creature looked similar in size and shape to Neely. Then it started to sing. The loud music vibrated the ball where Ajax sat.

His eyes darted around in a nervous frenzy, hoping that this ancient relic would be able to withstand the trauma.

Within a few moments several other silver creatures swam forward from various directions. They didn't appear hostile, but they flanked Neely on each side.

Ajax watched, wondering what magic he could do down here if the fish became aggressive.

They swam over a long wall of coral and Ajax couldn't believe his eyes. A city, grander than any he'd laid eyes on, sprawled out before him. Encompassed in a large dome that looked to be created from the same material as his globe, it looked as though it spanned on forever.

Inside the dome, bright-colored structures filled the streets. Off in the distance rose a golden glimmering castle. In between the buildings grew large leafy plants in turquoise, dark purple, and vibrant orange tones.

They dove toward the bottom of the cavern where a long tube stretched outward. Some of the silver fish, that Ajax now assumed to be mermaids, entered first, followed by Neely, and a few more trailed behind Ajax.

Once inside the tube, a large door closed and the water receded. When the water had all been evacuated, the giant fish shook off the last remnants of the ocean from their scales and transformed into merpeople.

All these mermaids had a silver coloring, but other than the color difference, they transformed like Neely, appearing in silvery clothes that matched their skin tone.

To Ajax's surprise, some were male, appearing in silvery trousers and tunics. All bowed before Neely, who looked stunned.

Ajax untied his restraints and pushed open the door to the ball he had ridden in. However, before he could take a step out, three of the men stood in front of him armed with daggers, looking ferocious.

"Stop! Leave him alone," Neely called.

The mermen stepped back and lowered their weapons, but their faces didn't mask their distrust.

Neely pushed through the merpeople who still knelt, and reached for Ajax, helping him out of the ball.

"What's going on? Why are they bowing to you, Neely?" Ajax asked, looking to her for answers.

Cold steel pressed against his throat before Ajax could register what happened.

"You shall address her as Your Majesty," the merman instructed, a cold glare in his eyes.

"Your Majesty?" Ajax asked, stunned.

The merman must have thought Ajax used the word to address Neely for he stepped back and lowered his dagger.

"Majesty?" Neely echoed. "What do you mean? I'm not royalty."

The merman who had held a knife against Ajax's throat moments before turned towards Neely. All hate vanished from his eyes, replaced with awe.

"We have been waiting so long for your return. We began to doubt anyone of royal blood would ever return."

"I'm not of royal blood," Neely said, shaking her head in disbelief and looking towards Ajax, as if he had answers.

"There is no denying it; the color runs through you," he said. "We will bring you to the royal counsel. They have been keeping the peace since you left."

"I shall come but I want you to leave Ajax be. He is my trusted friend. Do not raise a weapon to him again," Neely said. "And before I see this counsel, we require medicine. Do you have healers?"

"Of course, Your Majesty," the merman bowed. "Forgive me for not noticing your injuries sooner, I was just so overwhelmed. I am Bolin. Please follow me, Your Majesty."

Neely shared an uncertain glance with Ajax. He shrugged and took a step towards her but stumbled from exhaustion.

Bolin waved two men over. They pulled Ajax to his feet and draped his arms on their shoulders to help support him.

Neely limped forward but waved off the offer of assistance when Bolin tried to send others to aid her.

"I'm not as injured as my friend."

A door slid open at the end of the tunnel. Ajax looked up as they entered a pebbled path into the city. He wondered how he could breathe down here. Could it be a sort of magic?

Merpeople went about their business shopping, working, chatting with one another. Merchildren played in a square a game that Ajax did not know.

As they made their way down the street a ripple of silence unfolded. One by one at first, and then several at time, the merpeople fell to their knees at the sight of Neely, expressions of awe and disbelief showed on their faces. Even the children fell silent.

Ajax peered up at Neely, who looked uncomfortable from all the attention.

At last they arrived at the structure that Ajax assumed to be the castle. Its golden spires reached high above all other buildings. Two soldiers manned the entrance, and at the sight of the newcomers, one scurried inside.

"Can it be?" the soldier that remained asked as he offered a low bow.

"Our prayers have finally been answered," Bolin said. "Send for our top healers. I shall escort them to the infirmary. Then call for the council to be convened. Our queen has returned."

Words could not express how wonderful it felt to be lying down on a soft bed. His injuries must have been extensive since his magic had not been able to heal them all thus far. The healer gave him something to drink that made him sleepy as she tended to his various wounds. It may also have had numbing properties because all his pain faded away.

Neely sat on a bed across the room from him surrounded by healers. Bolin tried to insist she go to private chambers for her own healing, but she insisted on staying to see how Ajax fared. The last thing he heard before sleep took him was Neely insisting that she did not need all of this attention.

His eyes felt heavy. Ajax blinked a few times as the room around him came into focus. It took him a moment to remember what had happened. He stretched his legs and it surprised him that he felt no soreness or achiness in them.

Ajax pushed himself into a sitting position, folded the blanket he'd been given, and began to examine his wounds. It amazed him. Only faint markings remained from where the vampire bats had attached to him. If he hadn't known where to look, he might have missed them completely.

Whatever had been in the tonic the healers had given him had done wonders. He no longer felt fatigued but invigorated.

Ajax gazed across the room to Neely's bed to find it empty.

In fact, if not for him, the room would be empty. Three other beds lined the wall with a set of shelves between each bed. Colored bottles of ointments, bandages, and small plants filled the shelves.

It felt unnerving to wake up without Neely here. But surely nothing bad had happened. Their queen had returned after all. They would not let anything happen to her. Still, Ajax wanted to find her, and the sooner the better.

He hopped off the bed and noticed his socks and boots were gone. The cold tile floor made him shiver. Upon further inspection, Ajax noticed he wore clean trousers and a new tunic. He hoped Neely had not witnessed them changing him. At least he had no memory of the incident.

Ajax made his way toward an archway he assumed to be the exit. There didn't appear to be any doors. In fact, when they arrived at the castle, Ajax couldn't recall seeing a single door. Even the main entrance had just been a large archway. Did the mermaids not care about privacy?

As he took his first step through the arch, two spears clanged in front of him. Ajax froze. Two soldiers wearing armor barred his path. At least it looked like armor, but instead of wearing it, the protective gear merged and became a part of them, similar to how Neely's clothes just materialized in the same coloring as her complexion.

"Where is Neely?" Ajax demanded.

Whack!

Ajax stumbled backwards, almost falling to the ground. One of the soldiers had backhanded him across the face. His cheek stung and anger welled inside of him.

"You shall refer to and address the queen with the respect and deference she deserves," the soldier who hit him said.

He rubbed his tender cheek. Ajax missed his medallion. If he had been wearing that, then that soldier would have had a fun surprise. But maybe he relied on it too much. Could his reflexes be slowing because of that?

Ajax took a deep breath. As much as he wanted to put this soldier in his place using magic now, to lash out in anger might alienate the merpeople to his quest. He still needed their help to locate the glow flower.

"My apologies," Ajax said through gritted teeth. "I am not used to N—to my friend being royalty. How could I be? Even she did not know. Can you please take me to her Royal Highness?"

The soldier stared at him in disbelief.

"If the queen wants to see you, she will summon you, not the other way around. No one makes demands of the queen. For now, you shall wait here. If you have need of food or drink, we will provide that for you at her bequest."

This came from the soldier that had not slapped him, although he looked as disgusted with Ajax as the other guard.

Neely knew they were on a time constraint. He would just have to trust that she remembered that throughout all this fanfare. If he didn't see Neely in the next two hours, then he would resort to other means to find her.

The time passed slowly. With nothing to occupy his time, Ajax at last asked for some food and drink to be brought to him. He needed to keep his strength up.

As Ajax dug into his second plate of food that consisted of some sort of sea creature and what he thought might be a vegetable, Neely strode into the room.

Her appearance had changed so much since he last saw her that Ajax dropped his fork in surprise. Neely looked regal. No one would doubt she was the queen.

Still the same shade of blue-green as always, Neely now wore a stunning ballgown that was, well, the exact shade as the queen, just like her other dress had been. Atop her head sat a golden tiara, with a giant heart-shaped diamond in the center and smaller emerald-cut diamonds on the sides. Stunning brilliant blue sapphires lined the top of the tiara, with hundreds of smaller princess-cut diamonds making an intricate weave throughout the tiara. She wore her hair up, something he'd never seen her do before. But he couldn't deny that she looked stunning.

"Your Majesty," Ajax said, offering as much of a bow as he could manage from a seated position.

Neely turned to her entourage and waved them away. "I need a moment alone with my friend."

"But Your Majesty," a mermaid began, "your guards aren't

to leave your side."

"They may wait outside. Ajax has been my protector for a long time; I trust him completely."

The mermaid gave Ajax a scathing look that told him that she didn't think he could protect anyone.

"You look the part," Ajax said, admiring Neely's new look.

Neely moved towards him. "It still feels rather bizarre. I don't know if I'll ever get used to it. I tried to explain that one of my siblings or parents would be more suited for this role. But they said if I'm the youngest female in the family then I am the rightful queen." She shook her head. "I don't think I can do this. My family has been away for so long. We know nothing of their traditions or customs. How can I lead when I do not even know my people?"

"You can," Ajax said. "You shall be the most remarkable ruler they have ever known. You have an extraordinary heart, and that is the most important attribute any ruler should seek. The rest you'll learn with time. I'd be happy to live under your rule."

"Be careful what you say. I may take you up on that. I feel so alone here." Then she took a moment to really look at him. "Are you feeling better?" Neely asked. "You look better."

"Much. I don't know what they used, but I'd like to bring some back to Rastella when this is all over." Ajax pushed his plate to the side and stood. "We need to find the magical glow flower and get back."

"That's what I've been doing while you slept. Asking questions and learning about this world. I found out where the flower grows but collecting it will be a treacherous mission."

"Of course it will be." Ajax sighed. "I guess I shouldn't be surprised. Nothing ever comes easy, does it?"

"I'm afraid not. But go ahead and finish eating and I will tell you what I've uncovered."

He picked up his plate and took another bite.

"The flowers grow solely along the sides of a cavern, but there is a ginormous creature that lives at the bottom. It eats sea life but loves mermaids. None will go near it. It can't stand the warmer water so it never leaves the cavern."

"Maybe it doesn't like humans. Regardless, I have to find some way to get it."

"I know," Neely agreed. "I've been racking my brain. I've been able to come up with one idea and even it sounds insane."

"Let's hear it."

She laid out her plan to Ajax. She would swim him out in the globe with an extended chain, then lower him into the cavern while keeping herself high above in the warmer water. Then the tricky part comes into play. Ajax would need to exit the globe quickly, hopefully exiting before it fills with water, Then he must cut the plant off the cavern wall, swim back to the globe, and enter it, again closing the door quickly before the globe fills with water. .

"How long can you hold your breath if the globe fills?"

Neely asked.

"I'm not sure, a couple of minutes maybe. I've never timed myself," he said. "Maybe I'll be able to breathe in the globe even with the water. I think it must have some magical properties. Otherwise the air would have run out on our journey here."

Neely sighed. "I wondered about that to...after we arrived," she gave him an apologetic glance, "but it doesn't. The colored plants in the globe are oxygen-producing plants. They provide air to the globes and even the entire city. That's why they grow all over the streets."

"Well, I'll just have to be fast enough," Ajax said.

After all, Nivara's life, and maybe everyone else's, depended on him. If he didn't bring back the plant and make the elixir then Nivara would die. And if he didn't come back, Blake, Leif, and Sky would still try to rescue Niv on their own. He had to succeed. No other option existed.

CHAPTER XX

Blake

As they crested a small hill and gazed down across the elven city, it looked as if they stepped into another world. It was so vastly different than the treacherous bogs they had just encountered. The children played and sang as older elves worked in gardens and mothers hung washing or stirred pots of stew.

Paved streets intertwined between modest homes. Blake would have expected to find this in a story book.

He never imagined elves living like this. He imagined them being born with swords in their hands, being taught of their superiority, and ripping into raw meat with their teeth. This looked…normal, even paradisiacal.

As they descended the path down into the town the elves started to take notice of them. Children stopped playing. Women froze mid-stir and the older male elves disappeared into their homes. Within moments the adolescent males returned, each armed. They marched towards Blake and his companions.

Leif placed his palm on Blake's chest, stopping him.

"Let me speak. They might listen to me," Leif said.

"Sounds good to me. I'll just stay back here and protect the prince," Sky said, springing from Leif's shoulder to Blake's.

Leif took a few more steps forward with his hands outstretched. "We mean you no harm."

The dark-haired elves stopped, eyeing Leif with suspicion. They ranged from a few years younger than Leif to several years older.

"Did Lord Striker send you?" one asked, stepping forward.

"Why would he send an elf with a human?" another elf hissed.

Blake wondered what Leif would say. Telling them that Striker had not sent them would only intensify the situation.

"I came to see for myself," Leif said, then paused as more members from the village made their way forward, curiosity painted on their faces. One beautiful woman stared at Leif with such an intensity it made the elf shiver.

"See what?" the first elf asked.

"The elf mothers," Leif said.

"Who are you?" the second elf asked.

"My name is Leif."

The woman who stared with such intensity let out a gasp. "It can't be true." She pushed through the crowd that gathered until she stood directly in front of Leif.

"It is you," she said, reaching up and stroking his cheek. "You're alive. How are you alive? Where have you been?"

Leif took a step back and stared into the woman's eyes, wishing he could remember her.

"Who are you? How do you know me?" he asked.

"You are my son," she said, throwing her arms around him. Then she pulled back and cupped his face in her hands. "Even though it can't be. You died years ago. You were murdered," she said, shaking her head in disbelief.

Leif looked shaken. Blake had heard the stories from Leif and Sliver, how Lord Striker had convinced the elves that there were no female elves. That babies came from the bogs, whether they fell from the sky or sprouted out from the ground, Blake didn't understand. Only Striker's most high-ranking officers traveled to the bogs with him on a yearly basis. That's where they'd collect young elves. It still seemed insane that Striker could convince the majority of elves that they just popped into existence, but they were taught it since as long as they could remember.

"How do you know that you are his mother? Many elves are taken from here when they are too young to remember. How can you be so certain?" Blake asked. He didn't want Leif's hopes to get raised for no reason.

"I know my son. Leif is the eldest child of myself and Lord Striker," she said, her voice cracking as she tried to contain her emotion. "I can still see my baby when I look at him. But if my word is not enough to convince you, and I can see that it is hard for my son to accept as well, I can show you proof. The female's bloodline is the strongest in our people. We each bear our own mark. That mark is passed down to each of our children." She turned her head and bent back her ear so Blake could see. "Leif will have the same mark, as do all of my children."

Blake examined the mark and then checked behind Leif's ear. They matched.

"It is true," he said, nodding to Leif.

"Mother," Leif said.

She came forward and embraced him in a long hug. This time Leif wrapped his arms around her too and pressed his forehead on hers. "I have a mother," he said, sounding awed.

Blake wondered if Leif had ever been hugged growing up. He doubted Striker embraced anyone.

"There is more to this story." She turned to her people. "This is my son and his companions. I shall speak to them alone. There is more to be learned here."

She turned back towards her son and his friends. "I am Nalva. Please accompany me. I need to know more. Things are not making sense to me."

Nalva led them down through the village until they reached a small stone home with several wooden chairs and a large table in the main room. It reminded Blake of the Maxwells' home.

After they took seats, Nalva brought them some clear, cold water and set cheese, bread, and small fish on the table.

Sky wasted no time digging in.

"Now, explain to me how you are not dead," Nalva said.

"Tell me first why you thought me dead. Then it will help me know where to begin."

Nalva nodded and unfolded her story to them. She told of them leaving the Mer Realm and starting a life here. This place had more space for them and they built and thrived here. Her husband Striker sat on an elven council back then. He tried to convince others that they were not safe, that others had become jealous of their prosperity and that in order to protect themselves they needed to wage war with the other species to show their dominance and make the others back down.

Nalva told Leif and his companions how none of the other council members listened, how not even she, his own wife believed him They had seen no evidence of his claims, and believed they lived in a peaceful place. For decades Striker tried to convince them, but none of them paid him heed. Then one day while she and most of the other wives spent the day down by a small creek gathering water and doing laundry, an attack befell the city.

By the time they had returned, homes burned in raging fires and many elves had been killed. Nalva told them how Striker had been injured fighting them off, but that he had told her that a mersoldier had killed Leif in front of his eyes.

"Somehow they tricked your father into thinking they killed you. But if they didn't, where have you been?" Nalva asked, stroking his hand and looking overjoyed at his return.

"Father lied to you," Leif said.

"No, they tricked him," Nalva said. "If he knew you were alive nothing would have stopped him from getting you back. He would have died trying."

"No." Leif shook his head sadly. "I have grown up in the home of my father. I lived with him this entire time and he never mentioned you. In fact, I grew up thinking we sprouted out of the bogs. Most of us do not know we have mothers, other than the few soldiers he must bring when he visits, to help repopulate our people. He is evil."

Nalva recoiled her hand. "That can't be true. You must be confused. He'd never keep you from me."

Leif rose from his chair, angry now. "He is a monster. He hates everyone and everything. I was never good enough. He hunts down those weaker than himself and attacks them. All he cares about is power. In the realm my friend Blake comes from," Leif said, pointing to the prince, "my father murdered men, women, and children. Innocent people who knew nothing of him and did naught wrong."

"It's true," Sky said. "If you step outside of this bog, elves are seen as evil creatures because of Lord Striker. He makes them commit atrocities. The creatures of this world loathe him but are terrified to do anything."

"He has taken the girl I love," Blake said, speaking the words aloud for the first time. "I am terrified of what he shall do to her. He has demanded we find ingredients to create an ancient potion that will make him invincible. He wants to rule over everything. I think he put you here to keep you out of the way."

"I need time to think about this," Nalva said, taking a bite of a hard cheese.

"You mentioned siblings? I have brothers and sisters?" Leif asked.

"You have two younger sisters and a younger brother. But you should have met your brother already. Striker brought him to Elf City months ago."

"I left Father a while ago. I could not stand to be with someone who solely wanted to cause pain. Father cares for none save himself. If he finds me, he shall kill me," Leif said.

"This is all so much. I do not know what to believe."

"Remember who has already lied to you. I cannot forgive Striker for keeping me from my mother for so long. Perhaps it is not the same for you." Leif's voice came out cold and unfeeling. "Take what time you need but we cannot stay here," he added.

Nalva's face saddened as she watched her son.

How could she even doubt Leif? Striker had lied to her about her son's death, yet here he stood. What other proof did she need?

Blake wondered if Leif would be okay. Meeting his mother had been a dream, but Blake doubted that Leif ever thought his mother would question his words. To have her give Striker the benefit of the doubt after all he had done to Leif couldn't be easy.

Perhaps with a little bit of time Nalva would be able to make sense of all this. Her world was shattered just like her son's.

"We have to get to the Animal Realm," Blake said. "There is a portal here. Can you show it to us?"

"Already?" Sky asked, stuffing his cheeks full of cheese.

Leif's mother shook her head. "No. I vowed never to show it to anyone. There are dangers in the other realms. Monsters that would kill you. I just got you back, my son. I cannot lose you a second time."

"There are monsters that would kill him here too," Sky muttered.

Blake pushed his chair from the table. "Well, we know it's here. If you won't show us we will just have to find it ourselves."

Nalva shrugged. "You are welcome to search, but you will not find it. And none of my people will assist you."

"Mother, please, I beg you. The life of a friend is at stake," Leif pleaded.

"I cannot put you in danger. I am sorry," Nalva said, but her expression did not waver.

"Let's split up," Sky suggested. "We can cover more ground that way."

Sky headed north of the marsh while Leif searched to the east and Blake the west.

After an hour they met back up outside of Nalva's home.

Blake looked hopefully at the others. "Did you find it?"

"No," Leif said.

"The island is not that big. I don't know where it could be hiding...unless..." Sky trailed off.

"Where? Do you have an idea?" Blake asked.

"You don't think it's hidden in the bottom of the Stinking Bogs?" Sky asked.

"No, it can't be..." Blake said, his eyes turning towards the direction of the bogs.

"Uhh..hmm," a small voice called from behind a tree.

Blake turned to see a younger girl elf, motioning for them to come to her. She appeared to be hiding.

"Should we go?" Sky asked.

"What do we have to lose?" Leif said.

As they made their way forward, the young elf ran up and over a small hill. They followed behind her as she hurried to an area covered in a dense fog.

She paused at the edge of a thin mist.

The heat grew more intense as they came closer.

"It's in there. But be careful," the girl said.

"What's in there?" Blake asked.

"The portal," the girl said, as she glanced around, looking to make sure no one saw her.

"I came this direction but it was so hot and I couldn't see anything," Sky said. "I guess I should have looked harder."

"Why are you helping us?" Leif asked.

"You said your friend was in trouble. I was eavesdropping outside the window."

"Why?" Blake asked.

"Because I wanted to see my brother."

"You are my sister?" Leif asked. "What is your name?"

"I'm Malva."

"I am Leif."

"I know that, silly. I was listening. Plus mother talks about you often. We all thought you were dead. So maybe nothing scary lives in the other realms. But be careful. I want you to come back. I want to learn all about your adventures and about the people you know." Malva turned to look over her shoulder. "I have to go. Make sure you time it right." She gave Leif a quick hug and then ran off.

"Time what right?" Sky called, but Malva never turned back around.

Suddenly the ground began to shake.

"What is that?" Leif asked as they headed into the fog.

As they made their way forward, the earth continued to tremble. Then a loud noise sounded in front of them and sprinkles of hot water rained down on them.

"Ow!" Blake said as he tried to shield his face.

Sky ran under the elf's tunic.

"It is burning hot!" Leif cried.

When the rain stopped, Blake looked to the others.

"I know what it is. It's a geyser."

"A what?" Sky asked.

"I have never seen one but have read about them. Hot water shoots up from beneath the ground periodically," he explained.

"Is that where the portal is?" Sky asked.

"I guess that is what my sister meant about timing. We must have to jump in between blasts," Leif said.

"Let's find the geyser and then we will wait until it erupts again. Once it's finished, we will have to hurry before it goes off again," Blake said.

They didn't have to wait long before water shot out of the hole in the ground. They covered their faces the best they could and waited until the geyser stopped.

"Run!" Leif yelled, jogging Blake out of his trance.

The ongoing eruptions made the ground muddy. Blake did his best to go his fastest without slipping. They slowed as they reached the edge of the geyser. It still steamed and the temperature grew hotter as they made their way closer.

Blake peered down into the hole, the steam burning his face. "I can't see anything but steam." He turned to Leif.

"I cannot be certain; there is so much steam. Sky, what do you see? You have the best eyesight of us all," Leif said.

Sky perched on Blake's shoulder, leaned forward, and peered down.

"You've got to be kidding me…of all the places…this is ridiculous."

"We'd better hurry then. We don't want to jump when the geyser starts up again," Blake said.

Leif adjusted his gear and turned to leap into the hole, but Blake grabbed him by the shoulder.

"You're not coming," Blake said.

"I have to. Niv needs our assistance."

"Sky and I can do this. You need to stay here with your mom and your sisters."

"No—" Leif began, but Blake pressed on.

"I've been thinking about this. Leif, if we give this elixir to Striker and he becomes invincible then the only way to stop him is to get the elves to turn on him. Striker trained his army well. They are vicious and skilled. But the elves here are different. They haven't been tainted by his evil to the same extent. Get them on our side. The right side. You can do this."

"He's right. We need more allies and you need to get to know your family. If you can convince them to join us, then the other elves will see the lies Striker has told them. It's our best option."

Leif paused, but that was all Blake needed.

“Good luck,” Blake said, patting Leif once on his back before grabbing Sky in an embrace, wrapping his cloak around them, and leaping into the steaming geyser.

CHAPTER XXI

Nivara

Boredom became Niv's constant companion, but in light of the torture and pain she expected, she welcomed it.

The same elf brought her food twice a day, always the same meal: a hunk of bread, an apple, and some type of cooked fish.

But it hadn't poisoned her thus far, and she couldn't detect any mold on it, so she ate it all. The bread always tasted a little stale and the apple had a bruise or two, but for prison food it tasted far better than she expected.

Her stomach rumbled. It must be close to mealtime, although being stuck in a cell all day made it hard to keep the time and days straight. If not for the meals, Niv could see how she might not even be able to tell day from night. She'd tried to entertain herself but she didn't have much to work with. She counted the stones that made up the cell several times, but since the number never changed, she grew tired of that rather fast.

1,963 stones.

She counted the straw in her cell, shifting it from one corner to the next, but ended up losing count.

Most of the time she thought about Blake and hoped he didn't put himself in danger attempting to rescue her.

The ground trembled slightly. The troll must have been called to open her door. A moment later the door opened and her usual elf came in bringing a tray of food.

"Good evening," Niv said, smiling.

Leif told her once that elves lived their lives with little kindness being bestowed upon them. Striker gave them none, and most elves worked and trained on a strict regimen leaving little time for anything else. Their leader also filled their heads with crazy ideas about how ruthless and mean other species were. So Niv decided to show this elf, and any elf she came into contact with, that Striker lied.

The elf didn't say anything when he entered, but Niv could have sworn he'd repressed a smile.

"Well, don't you look dashing in your uniform today," Niv continued as if they conversed all the time.

The elf set the tray down on the floor and stopped.

Niv looked down at the tray and noticed something new on it. Today instead of just fish, bread, and an apple, there lay a small piece of cheese.

"Something new today," Niv said, giving him an appreciative smile. "Thank you… I still don't know your name."

"Stepin," the elf said before turning and scurrying out of the room.

If she didn't know any better, Niv could have sworn Stepin had blushed. Maybe she had made some headway after all.

The door slowly began to close but stopped halfway. Then the ground trembled as the troll departed.

Unsure of what to expect, Niv waited for a few moments. Just as she had convinced herself to peer out the door, Telkin stepped inside the cell.

"Please, eat," Telkin said, gesturing to her uneaten tray.

"To what do I owe the pleasure of your company?" Niv asked.

She hadn't laid eyes on him since he had brought her down here and locked her away.

"You found your manners," Telkin noted. "Perhaps this is just a trick. You seem to have bewitched Stepin. I see contraband on your tray."

"Please don't do anything to him. Take the cheese but don't hurt him," Niv said, worried that she may have gotten the elf into trouble.

"Why do you care what happens to him? He's your jailer. He helps keep you locked away," Telkin said, staring at her with such intensity she turned her gaze from him.

"There is kindness in him. Perhaps not all elves are evil. Maybe I've just come into contact with the worst of your kind," Niv said, eyeing him warily.

"I've been making inquiries. I wonder if you can explain a couple of things to me," he said, then paused, waiting for an answer.

"I shall have to hear the question before I can answer that."

"Why do most elves believe that there are no female elves? The fact in itself is absurd. It doesn't even make sense." Telkin rubbed his chin and looked deep in thought.

"Because Striker lies. Have you not caught on by now? I don't know how many elves know the truth. Some must, if elf babies keep being born."

"But how could anyone believe a lie like that?"

Niv shrugged. "If you're taught something since birth and everyone around you is taught the same thing, why would you question it? None of these elves have ever seen a female elf. Striker keeps them all locked away somewhere. Why would he let Leif's brother and mother and sisters think him to be dead? Striker does nothing unless it's to his own benefit."

"Father told me to be careful around you. He says you're dangerous. That lies drip from your tongue and you can bewitch those around you."

Niv laughed, a loud real laugh.

"And you wondered how your brother could believe that female elves didn't exist."

She stepped forward and picked up her tray, then took a bite of bread as Telkin watched her.

"Why did you come here, if I'm a skilled liar that can

enchant you? And if that's the case, why haven't I used this magic to procure my escape?"

Telkin didn't answer.

Niv took a bite of her cheese. She had not realized how much she missed variety.

"Why don't you go investigate some more? Find out how many times in all these years the elves have seen another creature or species raise a finger against your people. Or better yet, how many lives the elves have taken in their quest for domination. Peace will never exist with Lord Striker leading your kind. The answer to your question, to all your questions, is staring you in the face. You just don't want to see it."

"You know something, I don't find any value in these visits of ours. I see no point in continuing them." Telkin stormed out of the room, looking a little more rattled than his previous visit.

At least he didn't just accept things at face value. Telkin asked questions and dug for the truth. He didn't turn a blind eye and believe everything Striker fed him. Leif did have a brother. Now she knew it hadn't been a lie.

CHAPTER XXII

Ajax

The globe sat in front of Ajax, ready for him to enter and strap himself in. Bolin had volunteered to bring him to the cavern. The council had been in an uproar at the idea of their queen doing something so dangerous.

Shouldn't the queen be the one making all the decisions? Perhaps it would take time for Neely to establish her authority. Ajax knew she'd make an excellent queen with time. At least she'd been able to learn the location of the flower and devise a strategy.

He'd have felt better if Neely took him to the cavern. He trusted her. Bolin on the other hand, Ajax knew nothing about. Would he panic at the first sign of trouble?

At least he volunteered in Neely's place. That showed some loyalty and bravery. He'd cling to that. Despite Bolin's apparent dislike for Ajax, his loyalty had to be admired.

Not knowing anything about the plant or the location he would soon enter, Ajax had opted to bring a sharp knife for cutting and a long spear in case he came face to face with the Shaddock. Aside from being a giant monster, Ajax learned that the Shaddock had six razor sharp tentacles and shot electric bolts out of its mouth to stun its prey.

Ajax took a deep breath before entering the globe. He strapped himself in and prepared himself as best he could for the moment the ball would shoot forward.

The tunnel opened up and water bubbled up around the outside of his shell.

Then without warning, Bolin shot forward. A few other mermaids flanked his side but as they neared a darker section of water, they slowed down and then stopped, leaving Bolin and Ajax to continue on their own. The globe slowed as they drew nearer to the dark cavern. Ajax spotted patches of a glowing purple light in the midst of the darkness.

As they drew nearer to the dark cavern Ajax spotted patches of a glowing purple light.

Those must be the glow flowers, Ajax thought.

He wished they grew closer to the surface of the cavern. The first flowers looked to be a few hundred feet down the rock wall. Neely lengthened the chain before they had left, but none of the mermaids knew how long the chain needed to be. They avoided this area.

Nothing short of the queen's request would bring them here.

Bolin swam high above the cavern and hovered as Ajax sank lower. He wondered if the Shaddock could already sense him. What he wouldn't give to have his medallion back at this moment.

The darkness encompassed him, but strangely the lower he descended the better he could see. His eyes must have been adjusting to the lack of light.

He hoped Bolin could see when to stop. A purple glow came from just below the globe as the orb stopped moving. Ajax unstrapped himself as quickly as his hands could manage. He took a deep breath and reached for the door when he felt the water shake around him.

The creature was on the move.

With no time to waste, Ajax gulped in his last lungful of air and shoved the door open. It took much more effort to push the door open underneath the water. He jumped out and pushed the door closed, kicking with his legs to propel himself forward.

Ajax didn't spare a moment to look at how high the water level rose inside his globe. He turned toward the purple plant and swam with all his might.

The cavern wall shook and Ajax saw blue eyes shining below him, moving in a frenzy up the wall. He was amazed by how fast the giant creature moved.

Whipping out his knife, Ajax sliced the plant off of the rock. He swiped a second time and a third, shoving the plants inside his shirt.

Lightning struck beside Ajax's head, notifying him that the time to depart had arrived. The sound boomed in his ear, singeing the edge. He felt disoriented but pushed off the rocks with his feet, knowing he needed to move before the next shot came.

He propelled himself through the ocean, making big strokes with his arms. It felt like he moved in slow motion as he made his way back toward his vessel. He didn't have the speed of the Shaddock. He'd never make it in time. Lightning shot forward from the beast, narrowly missing Ajax. His lungs ached, begging him to take a breath. Suddenly, a sharp pain tore through the bottom of his foot. A tentacle had lashed forward, raking the sole of his foot. In another second the creature would slash through him like a hot knife through butter.

He motioned his hand at the creature, sending him tumbling backwards with a magic wave. Ajax hoped this would give him enough time to get inside the globe, but with the pressure from the water and his weakened power with the medallion gone, the Shaddock didn't get thrown deep enough. It took seconds for the beast to recover and sprint forward with an ever-growing anger.

Ajax reached the door to the globe and flung it open using all his strength. He gripped the edge of the frame to pull himself in, knowing it would be too late. The Shaddock barreled towards him and Ajax had no time to react. The monster lashed a tentacle forward and Ajax closed his eyes, knowing this one was the end.

Suddenly Ajax was being ripped forward in the water. He opened his eyes and saw that Bolin had rammed himself into the creature, causing the globe and Ajax to be pulled after him. They thrashed against the rocks. Bolin, torn and bleeding, continued to fight.

The Shaddock swiped a tentacle at the mermaid, sending Bolin spiraling backwards. Ajax reached forward with his hand and used his magic to pull at the boulders scattered along the ridges of the cavern. One by one they started falling down until a cascade of rocks came lose. They hammered down one after the other pelting the Shaddock until he retreated.

Ajax's head felt fuzzy. He pulled himself into the orb, it felt like a lot of time had passed but it had probably only been a couple of minutes. The globe, now filled with water, had no pockets of air for Ajax to breathe. Blackness filled the corners of his vision, when an idea struck him. He used the rest of his strength and lunged upward, grabbing a leaf off of the plant growing in the orb and stuffed it in his mouth.

His fatigue started to fade and his energy came back as oxygen flooded his body. The plant that gave off oxygen somehow had the air inside it.

Bolin swam over in awkward movements, and Ajax gave him a thumbs up to get them out of this cavern.

As the mermaid pulled them back towards the city, Ajax continued to cut off pieces of the plant and consume them. It felt a little odd to be eating the oxygen. But as he swallowed, the air dissipated from the plant and moved into his lungs. He just hoped that enough of the plant remained to last him the entire journey.

When they at last arrived at the tunnel, Ajax rushed to

Bolin's side as the water receded.

"Bolin, are you all right?" he asked as the fish creature shifted back into a human-like being, collapsing into Ajax's arms.

"I will be. I've survived worse."

Other mermen rushed into the tube and started attending to the soldier's injuries.

"Why did you risk your life for me?" Ajax asked. Bolin had radiated hostile vibes since the first moment they met. "I didn't think you even liked me."

"I don't." Bolin laughed and then winced as another merperson put pressure on a wound. "The queen asked me to protect you so I did. But you did surprise me." He gasped as they wrapped a wound in a tight bandage. "You saved me, too. I have never met a human. I didn't know if bravery existed among your kind."

"We need to get him back to the castle. We can treat him better there," one of the merpeople said.

Ajax stood back and let them pass by as they carried Bolin out of the tube. Ajax hoped they administered the same tonic to his new friend as they had given him when he first arrived.

"Her Majesty has requested that you be brought to her as soon as you returned," a mermaid said after the soldiers carried Bolin out.

"Of course," Ajax said, following after the woman.

"So how long have you known the queen?" the lady asked

as they walked.

"For a while," Ajax said, surprised someone chose to make conversation with him by their own accord.

"Have you seen any others of the royal family?" she asked, her eyes sparkling with excitement.

"No, I've just met Ne—" He stopped, catching himself in time. "Only Her Majesty." It still felt odd to call her that. Now he'd have to bow to two of his friends. Although for some reason it didn't bother him quite as much with Neely.

Ajax did have to admit when he first found out about Nivara and Blake's engagement, he felt upset. He didn't want to see his best friend forced into a marriage of convenience, however comfortable it might be for her. But as time passed, he couldn't deny what he'd seen with his own eyes. Blake loved Nivara and he'd do anything for her. She made him a better person. And Ajax suspected Niv had begun to feel the same way. She always defended him and wasn't afraid to speak her mind with him, regardless of how upset her views might make him. His title didn't intimidate her. Ajax had worried that because of his title, she might never be able to have a normal relationship with him. But he'd been wrong.

"Well, it is so exciting to have her back," the lady exclaimed.

He followed her through a maze of hallways, and through five or six, small but beautiful gardens until they entered a library.

No doors were on any of the rooms he passed. Ajax assumed his guess had been right, and they did not exist.

The queen saw Ajax before he saw her.

"Did you get it?" Neely asked, knocking over a pile of books in a very undignified manner as she rushed to greet him.

She slowed suddenly and walked in a more regal manner, perhaps noticing how she might look. Ajax noted a few of her advisors eyeing her closely. Royalty had many perks but Ajax did not feel certain that the incentives outweighed the expectations or the constant watching and judging that followed a royal wherever they went.

"Yes, I got them," Ajax said, pulling the flowers out of his shirt. "They are a little smashed," he noted, looking at the limp plants. "Hopefully that won't impact the elixir."

"While you were gone, I've been working with some of our archivers. There are journals and entries here about the portals and the different realms, as well as notes as to how the merpeople used to make their way through Never Ending Night."

"I didn't think the portal was moved there until after the elves took over. And that no one had gone through since."

"I'm not sure about all of it," Neely began as she pulled Ajax over to a pile of books. "There is so much here to go through. But from what I've pieced together, the royal family visited Lord Striker to try to broker some sort of peace. They gave strict orders that none were to follow. Something must have happened. The family, my family or my relatives, never returned. Despite the orders, the council sent two parties to search for the king and queen, but none returned. Perhaps the portal has always been there." Neely flipped through a journal and pointed to an entry. "I do know before everything went crazy between the elves and the rest of the realms, we used to travel back and forth. There is a special type of plant that grows in that forest. It has restorative properties. So my people used to go and scavenge for it. There is a shell that emits a soft glow, similar to the light we used to get through the forest, but for whatever reason the bats aren't drawn to it." Neely said, her face lit with excitement.

"And you have access to these shells?" Ajax asked while envisioning another dangerous mission in the foreseeable future.

"Piles and piles of them," Neely said with a sly grin.

"At last, a piece of luck," Ajax said, smiling for the first time since he could remember.

CHAPTER XXIII

Blake

The ground lay covered in sharp, jagged rocks but somehow Blake managed to land on his feet.

"A little warning next time would be nice," Sky said as he worked to catch his breath. "You almost gave me a heart attack."

"I offer you my sincere apology," Blake said. "But I couldn't give Leif time to change his mind. He needed to stay. And at least you didn't land on a pile of spiky rocks. My feet are killing me."

"No time for complaining. Now it's up to you and me. Did Ajax give you any ideas on where to start looking for the unicorn hair?" Sky asked.

"No. Which direction do you think we should go?"

He looked around. The portal swirled behind them. They stood on top of a large rocky hill. To the east lay snowy mountains for as far as the eye could see. To the west, Blake saw desert stretching for miles and miles. Behind them, the hill extended in a sharp incline, and in front of them, Blake could see a forest with a large lake embedded deep within the woods.

"I vote we head for the forest," Sky said.

"Why the forest?" Blake asked as he stepped down the

rocks, being careful with his footing.

"Because it's downhill," Sky said, pointing in the direction he wanted Blake to take them.

"There is also a lake down there. That's a good place for animals to drink."

A loud squawking sounded from above. Blake looked up and saw a large griffin flying overhead. He ducked down, hoping the large beast hadn't seen them.

"I know I shouldn't be surprised but I can't believe those are real," Blake said, staring in awe at the majestic creature.

"Let's not stand here discussing it. I don't know what those things eat. I thought a mountain lion big, but massive doesn't even begin to describe those griffins. We can make a plan once we are in the trees."

Sky leapt off of Blake's shoulder and scurried down the rock hill, never pausing or looking back until he rested, concealed beneath the canopy of trees.

It took Blake longer to make his way down the slope. The terrain made it difficult to find good footing.

"Thank you for waiting," Blake said when he entered the thicket.

"I just needed to stretch my legs," Sky said. "I've been riding on shoulders a lot lately."

Blake raised an eyebrow. "Oh, is that so? Then perhaps you want to shift forms and let me ride you for a while. It will help you exert some more energy."

Sky turned and peered into the woods. "Tempting as that is, I think my larger size would draw too much attention. Seeing the size of that griffin makes me wonder about the predators here."

Blake laughed. "Fine. But I hope you've never shifted into a griffin before. Because that would be a nice way for us to get out of here in a flash if needs be."

"Let's worry about that later. First, we need to find a unicorn."

Nothing stirred in the forest aside from the rare breeze shifting the leaves. The trees grew together in a dense manner and stretched to the heavens, making their journey challenging and slow.

As they moved deeper into the forest the trees thinned and Blake caught sight of a couple of smaller animals. Each darted off the moment they saw Blake and Sky.

One looked similar to a rabbit, but double the size, and with wings that reminded Blake of a dragonfly. The other creature they encountered had a reptilian appearance, but before Blake could get a good look, the creature burrowed down into the ground, swishing its long snake-like tail as it disappeared.

"A human," something cawed from above.

Blake's eyes rose to find the voice that had called to them. His hand reached for his sword on instinct, and Sky scurried up to perch on his shoulder.

A large black-feathered bird hung upside down on a branch

twenty feet above their heads. The bird's neck twisted at an unnatural angle to look at them. Its massive talons looked oversized for the creature and sunk deep into the bark.

"I can't remember the last time a human ventured to our realm," the bird continued. "Have the elves at last fallen?"

"You know about the elves?" Blake asked.

"Of course. They tried to ruin everything, but a sorcerer moved the portal on the other side so the elves couldn't find it. No one has ventured through since. On either side. We have little interest in what goes on over there."

"We are trying to stop the elves. But we are in need of assistance. We need the hair of a unicorn."

"Unicorns don't like the forest. They enjoy the cold and the mountains." The bird cawed and sat up straight on the branch, stretching its long wings. "I don't know why I'm telling you that. You won't be around to find one."

Before Blake or Sky had a chance to ask what the creature meant, the bird dropped from the branch, diving towards them. His beak opened wide, revealing rows of needle-sharp teeth as it barreled towards them, strong talons extended.

Blake dropped to his knees as the bird narrowly missed the top of his head. He drew his sword as Sky leapt to the ground shimmering, transforming into his largest size.

The bird circled around and dove again, screeching an ear-splitting sound. The noise incapacitated Blake, causing him to drop the sword as his hands flew to his ears.

The bird's talons raked across Blake's shoulders, and he cried out in pain.

"Get on!" Sky yelled as the bird prepared to descend upon them again.

Blake threw himself onto Sky and the hoosula dashed off through the trees.

Loud screeching followed as they wove in between the trees.

His arm throbbed, making it hard to stay on Sky's back, but he tightened his good arm on a handful of fur and prayed he'd stay on.

"If we can get back to where the trees are denser, the bird will have a hard time following us," Sky yelled.

Risking a glance over his shoulder, Blake saw the bird gaining on them.

"This might be a good time to change into something else," Blake suggested. "It's getting closer."

"Not yet," Sky said as he hurtled forward. "Try flinging one of your knives at it."

The bird dove towards them. Blake pressed his knees into Sky's sides for balance and reached for a knife. As he raised his hand to throw it, a giant black lion leapt over them, snatching the bird in his jaw.

Blake lost his grip and tumbled off Sky's back. He rolled across roots and felt rocks digging into him, before smashing into a tree.

Knowing he failed Niv was the last thought Blake had as he looked death in the face. Pain lanced through his head as he stared into the eyes of an enormous black lion.

His back pressed against a tree, unable to reach a weapon, Blake knew he had moments left to live. At least Sky got away. He'd save Niv. Blake would hold onto that as his last comforting thought.

"He's awake," the lion said, sniffing Blake and then taking a step back.

"Guess what?" Sky said, popping up from the top of the lion's mane. "He's a cambriar too!"

Blake groaned as he pushed himself up into a sitting position. He stretched out his arms and legs, amazed to find nothing broken. He wished he could say he felt no pain, but that would not be the truth. His shoulder felt the worst. He inspected it quickly. The shallow scratches throbbed. With the pain he felt, Blake couldn't believe that they weren't deeper.

"He's like you?" Blake said, trying to sort out what happened.

"This is Jeda. You've been out for a while. That flying creature is called a screecher. I'm sure I don't need to tell you why. Nasty things. Anyway, we've been discussing things and I found out we are both cambriars. Lucky for us, Jeda changed shapes this morning. Yesterday he had been experimenting with life as a snail."

"You have my thanks," Blake said, rubbing the back of his head. "I don't suppose you can help us find a unicorn?"

Sky giggled.

"You won't believe this, but his sister is a unicorn. I mean, unless she's decided to shift since Jeda went hunting."

"That's unlikely," Jeda said, flipping his tail. "We try to give a new body three months before we try out something else. And Pipa has been in her body a month."

"You were a snail for three months?" Sky asked. "I don't think I could have lasted that long. I mean, talk about boring. And the food choices…well, they don't exist."

"I made it a month, and even that took sheer determination and will- power."

The two cambriars laughed.

"As happy as I am that you two have so much in common, can we go find this…Piii…"

"Pipa," Jeda said.

"Right, Pipa, and return home. Nivara needs us."

"Of course," Sky said. "But we also need to find a way to get home. I've been discussing our predicament with Jeda and he has some ideas."

Blake stood up and leaned against the tree for balance.

"What do you mean? We know how to get home; we just go back through the portal."

"And end up at the bottom of a geyser that could erupt any second."

"I hadn't thought of that," Blake said, leaning back against the tree and closing his eyes.

"Besides, I've been thinking, and the more species we have to go up against Striker with the better. I think Leif will bring around the elves in the bogs, but how will they be able to get to Elf City? I don't fancy fighting any more of those claw monsters," Sky said, then shuddered from the memory. "Striker uses langabeasts to visit the bogs. He's never had to fight those creatures. We need to find flying animals to help us and transport the elves to fight for us."

"Let's go find Pipa. On the way, you can fill me in on your ideas," Blake said, taking a step forward, his leg wobbling. "Would it be possible to get a ride?"

His body ached. Sky didn't like others riding him. He'd allow it in an emergency but felt it beneath his dignity at other times. Blake hoped the lion didn't feel the same.

"Surely, why not?" Jeda said, leaning low so Blake could climb on.

The softness of the lion's fur surprised Blake. He'd never touched anything like it before. Blake struggled to climb on the lion's back, using his uninjured shoulder to pull him up.

"My family's not far from here," Jeda said once the prince had adjusted himself to a comfortable position on the animal's back. "Hold on, I've never had anyone ride me before, so I'm not sure how this shall be."

Blake gripped the lion's mane with his good hand and used his legs to help him balance.

Sky sat in front of Blake, not looking worried in the least.

"This is so exciting. An entire family of cambriars," Sky exclaimed.

Jeda started off at a slow lumber, then increased his pace at gradual intervals. Soon they ran through the trees, the wind blowing in Blake's hair.

Riding on the back of the lion differed from riding a horse. On a horse the rider had more control; here Blake had none, but it felt exhilarating. The lion made little noise, his furry paws padding his leaps and bounds. Jeda didn't take a straight path either. He'd run, then bound up on a rock or fallen tree and jump to another area, then run some more and jump. Blake wondered if they could train the Rastellian lions to be ridden but thought better of it. The lions back home were smaller but more savage. The line of people wanting to try their luck on the back of one would be small.

A narrow stream ran beside them, and Jeda followed it until it opened up into a small pond surrounded by a meadow of colorful flowers and lush green grass.

Several creatures of varying sizes rested in the light, one of which caught Blake's attention. A silver unicorn lay sprawled out on a stone.

The size of the unicorn caught Blake by surprise. It couldn't have been much bigger than a mouse. In the stories he'd read, unicorns had been the size of horses, rideable.

A griffin lapped water up from the edge of the pond, while a tan and white snake lay coiled, snoozing in the grass. Two purple animals with white stripes, not much bigger than a pig, grazed on some pink flowers.

The animals paid the lion no mind as he slowed and walked to the pond. Jeda leaned down and Blake slid off his side. Sky hopped down after him.

At the sight of Blake, the purple and white animals grazing froze mid-munch, grass falling from their mouths.

"Is that a human?" the griffin asked, heading towards them.

"This is Blake," Jeda announced. "He and Sky," the lion said, waving a paw towards the hoosula, "traveled through the portal."

"It's been forever since anyone used the portal," the unicorn said.

Jeda's family made their way forward, their eyes full of curiosity.

"I've never met a human," the snake said, slithering over.

"Sky is a cambriar, just like us," Jeda said.

"There are cambriars on the other side of the portal?" the griffin asked.

"We must have gotten trapped there when the sorcerer hid the portal on the other side," Sky said. "I can't believe you are all like me. Have any of you found your true shape?"

"My parents have," Jeda said. "This is my father, Sim, and my mother, Gina."

The two purple and white animals stepped forward. "We encourage our children not to choose their forever shape until they find their mate. It makes things easier that way."

"How do you know when you meet another cambriar?" Blake asked. "If you can shift into any animal, how do you tell…" He almost asked how one could tell a real animal from a cambriar, but thought that might come out sounding rude. He couldn't think of a polite way to phrase his question.

"How do we tell if an animal is born into the species or if it's one of us, shifted?" Sim asked, reading Blake's mind.

"Exactly."

"There is no way to tell by looking. You find out as you get to know the animal," Gina answered.

"That's what makes it so difficult," Sky said.

"What brings you to our world?" the griffin asked. "I'm Mila by the way," she added.

"I need an ingredient for an elixir. If I don't get it, the girl I love will be killed."

Jeda's family gasped and looked horror-stricken.

"What is it?" Pipa asked.

"Funny you should ask," Sky said. "We need a hair from a unicorn."

"Really? What's so special about my hair?" She craned her neck around, looking at her mane and swishing her tail. "I suppose you can have one, although I'd prefer it from my tail."

"That is kind of you," Blake said. "I hate to ask, but would it be a terrible imposition if I took two? Our journey thus far hasn't been easy. We've lost some of our gear and supplies. It would be nice to have a backup."

"I suppose that would be okay."

He reached forward and plucked two strands out from her tail.

"Ouch," Pipa said.

"My apologies," Blake said, securing the strands in his bag.

"It's fine, it only lasted a second."

"So that's it, now you'll go back through the portal?" the snake hissed.

"Not quite," Jeda said. "They need our help. There are animals on the other side being persecuted. Cambriars have been forced into servitude. I think we should aid them."

"How can we help?" Sim asked.

"I know it's asking a lot, but Jeda said there are lots of cambriars here," Sky said. "If a cambriar feels like they have found their true form I would ask them to be excluded from my request. But our hope is that any cambriar willing, would shift into the form of a griffin or other flying beast capable of carrying someone."

"Yes," Blake said. "We left a friend on the other side to secure us more allies, but in order for any of them to assist us they shall need transportation back to Elf City. The path on foot is dangerous and we don't want to risk any lives if we can avoid it."

"They plan on taking on the elves and restoring peace and trade throughout the realms," Jeda said. "I've always wanted to meet a mermaid."

"Will you help us?" Blake asked, trying not to get his hopes up. "Gathering others who can fly would be a tremendous help, but even if you can't accomplish that, Mila, if you'd be willing, we need a ride back through the portal. If we don't fly back, it shall mean certain death for us."

"I shall aid you in any way I can," Mila vowed.

"We can't make any promises on who would be willing to accompany you, but we will spread the word," Gina said, nodding to her children. "Seema, you take the desert. Jeda, take the mountains..."

Before Gina could finish, the snake and the lion darted off in different directions.

"...Pipa, you take the forest, and Mila, you take the plains that lay beyond the portal."

"Thank you so much for your help," Blake said.

"I know time is of the essence, so I shall spread the word as fast as I can and then meet you at the portal regardless of whether or not I can gather any aid to your cause," Mila said as she flapped her long golden wings and took flight.

"We shall escort you to the portal," Sim said. "These woods can be dangerous. We can't fly and won't be able to travel with you through the portal, but at least we can make sure you get back safely."

"Safe is good," Sky said as he glanced back over his shoulder at the forest, probably remembering the bird creature that attacked them.

"Right, let's get going," Sim said, nodding to his wife.

The two furry creatures linked their front legs together and kicked up their back legs. Then they began to spin.

Blake hadn't noticed before, but they had sharp curved hooves instead of feet. As they spun, dirt sprayed around them, and Blake raised his arm to shield his eyes from the debris.

A moment later the animals stopped and a hole stood in the ground, leading to an intricate pathway of underground tunnels.

"Hop on down," Gina called. "This way will be much faster."

"And safer too," Sim added. "We've made tunnels all over the Animal Realm."

The dark tunnels made Blake hesitate. He didn't like going into places he couldn't see, but Sky hopped down and strode forward.

"These are amazing," Sky said.

Blake envied the animals and their superior eyesight. He jumped down, landing hard, the fall deeper than he thought.

It took everything in him not to groan out loud. The jump rattled his entire body, sending shooting pains through his shoulder. The rest of his body groaned in protest as he stepped forward into the dark.

Not even shadows were visible down here. Blake trailed his hand against the side of the tunnel to keep him centered and focused on the sound of the footsteps in front of him. The darkness didn't hinder the others. Sky kept up a jovial conversation with Sim and Gina as they led them deeper into the twisting tunnels.

He kept waiting for his eyes to adjust, but not even a sliver of light penetrated these walls. Blake wondered how far underground they were. At times the tunnels descended deeper beneath the earth. Other times Blake's legs ached at the steepness of the climb. But between the twisting bends in the tunnel and his disorientation from the darkness, Blake lost track of any idea of how deep they were.

"This should be it," Sim said after they had hiked for a while.

Blake felt Sky rub against his leg, and then felt a whoosh of air, followed by particles of dirt flinging at him.

Sim and Gina burrowed upward.

Blake shielded his eyes, and within moments light filtered down from a giant opening in the ground.

Warm rays greeted him when he removed his hand from his eyes. Climbing out proved to be more difficult. Blake couldn't reach the top. Sky climbed on the prince and scrambled up his outstretched arms. From there, Sky launched himself up using the extra skin under his arms to glide to a soft landing above.

Roots grew into the earth. Blake tugged on several that came out into his hand until he found one that felt sturdy. After tugging on it once more to be certain, he pulled himself up. Then, reaching a higher root, Blake used his other arm to grasp it. He made his way up to the surface in an agonizing climb. When he finally pulled himself up out of the tunnel, he collapsed in exhaustion.

Blood trickled down the slashes on his arm, his scabs bursting open from his exertion.

"Are you all right?" Sky asked.

"I won't be all right until I have Niv back," Blake said, pushing himself up and then pointing to his shoulder. "This is naught compared to losing her."

"Well, this ought to cheer you up," Sky said, a wry grin on his face.

"What?"

"Turn around." Sky motioned behind Blake towards the portal.

Pushing through his pain and exhaustion, Blake craned his neck around to look in the direction Sky pointed. A crowd stood behind him surrounding the portal, langabeasts, griffins, giant birds, and other flying beasts that Blake had never seen before.

Jeda lumbered forward. "I wish I could have brought more. There are many cambriars who wanted to help, but they've already locked into their permanent shape and can't fly."

"You've surpassed any expectations I had. Thank you."

"Just one more to add," the lion said before shimmering and shifting into a griffin like his sister Mila, only he was solid black. "I haven't flown in a while. Last time I flew, I took the shape of a small bird. Then I decided to try a snail. They looked interesting, but I didn't like being tiny, so I changed into a lion. I like being bigger but miss the freedom of taking to the skies."

"Would you mind if we flew back on you?" Sky asked, leaping onto the back of the griffin before he could respond.

"No, I was hoping I'd get the honor," Jeda said, kneeling down and lowering his wings so that Blake could climb up.

"Thank you again for your family's assistance," Blake said, waving at Gina and Sim. "Please thank them all."

"Good luck," they called back as Jeda took off in a sweeping glide through the portal.

Blake closed his eyes and prayed that the geyser would not be erupting when they flew through. Wind blew through his hair as Jeda flew. Then Blake felt them flying higher and risked a peek.

They made it through the portal safely. He had hoped some spell had been placed on the geyser to ensure that it didn't erupt when someone passed through the portal. After all, they had no way of knowing the timing of the geyser from the Animal Realm.

Blake felt a huge sense of relief when every cambriar flew

through the portal after them without incident.

CHAPTER XXIV

Nivara

Niv's hopes of escape dwindled the longer she stayed in the dungeon. She could find no weak points in the thick walls. Even if she could break the lock on the cell door, she'd have no way to get the door open. Now Stepin had been reassigned, or at least Niv hoped that explained his disappearance. The new soldier did nothing but glare at her each time he came into the cell. Not once had he acknowledged anything Nivara said, despite her best efforts to employ him in conversation.

Telkin had not visited again. Maybe she pushed him too hard. Leif's brother didn't appear to have the same hateful demeanor as his father. She hoped Stepin, the elf who brought her food, had not been punished for his kindness to her.

Niv had tried to reach out to Ajax with her mind, to convince him not to come after her, which she knew would be in vain, but the connection felt severed. Like it had when she first left Rastella. She felt nothing when she reached out to him.

Maybe he'd done the right thing and gone back home, found a way to seal the portal permanently. That's all Niv wanted, for her family and friends to be safe. Ajax couldn't be so stupid as to hand an elixir of invincibility to the evilest creature of the realms.

But when she put more thought into it, she wondered if she would leave Ajax here had their places been switched, never knowing what happened to him.

The hours between meals ticked by slowly. Squeak had been Blake's companion when he spent time in the elves' dungeon. Niv searched her cell from top to bottom but no cambriars resided in here with her.

The ground rumbled and Niv stepped away from the door. Within minutes the large door stood open. It felt too early for a meal. Her stomach rumbled before mealtime but made no sound now. Nivara started when Telkin stepped into the cell.

She thought she had seen the last of him. On his previous visit he insinuated that he would not be back. Yet here he stood.

Niv wondered what questions he'd ask her today. Or perhaps Striker, at last, convinced Telkin that she deserved torture.

"Tomorrow is the deadline. There's been no sign of my brother or your friends," Telkin said.

"What happens to me..." Niv began but stopped. Did she really want to know what Striker would do to her? If she only had twenty-four hours or less left, did she want to spend it dreading the way Striker plotted her demise? It would be slow and painful. The leader of the elves relished causing pain and it seemed to be some sort of sick bonus if it also caused his son

Leif to suffer.

"It's not pleasant," Telkin said.

"That's an understatement," she said, staring back defiantly. She would not allow them to see her cower, no matter how much the thought of what tomorrow would bring terrified her. "So, did you just come here to taunt me?" Niv asked, but before waiting for an answer she continued. "My friends will be here. They'll find a way to save me."

"No, they won't," Telkin said, reaching into his cloak.

Not waiting to see what the elf had planned for her, Niv jumped back, grabbed the one small stool in the cell, and gripped it tightly, ready to defend herself to the end.

Telkin stopped and stepped back. He put up his hands in a peaceful gesture.

"Your friends aren't going to rescue you because you won't need it. I'm going to get you out of here." He pointed to his cloak and pulled it open, then reached inside and pulled a bundle out.

It was another cloak, like Telkin wore. Like most of the elves wore.

Niv lowered the stool and set it back on the stone floor.

"My father has ordered most of his subjects to set up a perimeter around the castle. He doesn't think Ajax will be foolish enough to try anything but he wants to be prepared nonetheless. In the morning the guards will be tripled. I plan to sneak you out then."

Niv accepted the cloak from Leif's brother.

"Why are you helping me?" she asked.

"I've been busy these past few days. Really the past few months. I've seen things that I don't like. I don't want to hurt anyone. I want to protect my people but I can see my father enjoys hurting others. And you're right," Telkin said, letting out a long sigh, "things he's told me don't make sense. He's lied to us, his own people, his own son, his wife." He shrugged. "I still don't understand everything that is going on, but I don't believe you are a threat."

"You know your father will kill you if he catches you helping me? He will see it as a betrayal. He has tried to kill Leif."

"See, that's why I feel like I am doing the right thing. I've felt off since I came to live here with my father. I've tried to make excuses for things I've seen, but now that I've met you everything has changed." He pointed to Nivara and shook his head. "You know horrible things await you tomorrow. And yet you still try to warn me. Dissuade me from helping you. I finally feel like I'm making the right choice."

"Thank you," Niv said.

"I will have to be by my father's side for much of tomorrow. He is grooming me to lead. But a mutual friend will come and get you when the time is right."

"A friend of mine?" Niv asked, trying not to laugh. "I don't think so."

"Don't worry. I've got it taken care of," Telkin said, offering her a slight bow of his head before exiting.

Once he had gone, Niv sat on the stool flabbergasted. She couldn't believe that Telkin decided to help her. And she had no idea who this mystery friend could be.

Could Sky be here? She didn't think anyone else could sneak in and out of the castle without being noticed. But how would he summon the troll to get the door to open? Leif would know the castle better than anyone. But that would be stupid and risky to send him here. The most notorious elf in history would be easy to spot. How could Leif hope to get all the way down the dungeon and back out again without anyone noticing him?

She'd just have to trust Telkin and this mysterious friend. After all, she didn't have any better options. She didn't have any options at all.

She unfolded the cloak and examined it. For the first time since she arrived, she felt hope.

CHAPTER XXV

Ajax

Tomorrow was the deadline the two elf goons gave Ajax. He now had the glowing Mer flower. Blake retrieved the dragon eggshells and with any luck had also obtained the unicorn hair.

Now Ajax just needed to return through the portal, meet Blake and Sky at the tower, and make it to Elf City before the end of the day tomorrow.

That didn't sound difficult in the least. He laughed to himself. He had to find a way. Keep thinking positive. He would save Nivara.

Then a horrible thought struck him. What if Striker didn't give them the entire day tomorrow? What if he meant by noonday? Or at first light?

He looked over the contents spread across the table. Neely stood across from him making the finishing touches on a map to Elf City.

"Leif will know the way, but just in case something happens and you get separated."

"Yes, we have no time to lose. We can't afford to overlook even the smallest detail," Ajax said.

One by one he checked each item before stowing it in his

satchel: two glowing Mer flowers, one glowing shell, several dried fish, a loaf of bread, five apples, a hunk of cheese, and his waterskin.

"I wish I could accompany you," Neely said. "But the people are terrified of losing a royal after so many years without a true leader."

"I know. I understand. Thank you for sending Bolin and his unit with me. I'll miss you, but traveling with these highly trained warriors will help ensure I get to the elven city. We shall easily squash any creature that attacks us."

Ajax thought back to when he, Neely, Niko, and Spots fought a giant sandworm. He'd have died if not for his protective medallion. Even with his magic, the serpent creature struck fast and proved difficult to kill.

Who knew what other creatures they might encounter? Without his medallion, it felt good to be traveling with fighters.

Their first test would be when they returned through the portal. After seeing how quickly the vampire bats were attracted to the light, Ajax didn't feel fully confident that these shells produced light that didn't attract the bats, despite what Neely read in some ancient texts. Having a dozen mermen with him eased his mind some.

If they were anything like Bolin, at least Ajax knew they wouldn't be cowards and run away at the first sign of trouble.

"Did you have a chance to get those words translated?" Ajax asked. He had given her a small parchment with the words that he found on the elixir recipe in the keeper archives.

She set the pencil down and sighed.

"No, I'm afraid not. No one could read it. They said it had some similarities to an older language some of my people knew, but none could translate it. A couple of them speculated that it mentioned a number but they couldn't be sure."

"Thank you for trying."

Neely rolled the map up and passed it to Ajax, placing her other hand on his shoulder.

"Take care, my friend," she said, then pulled him in for an embrace. "When this is all over, find my family and send them home."

"I will," Ajax said, trying to sound sure. "You have my sincere gratitude for all your help. You are a true friend. I'm sure I will see you soon."

He hastily packed his bag and turned to face the archway. Bolin stood waiting, his soldiers lined up behind him.

"Let's go," Ajax said, striding towards Bolin.

Of all the things Ajax might miss about the Mer Realm, traveling inside a giant orb would not be one of them. The beauty of the ocean astounded him. He never imagined such color to lurk beneath the dark and foreboding surface. He couldn't quite enjoy the scenery around him though, as Bolin did not take as much care as Neely had when transporting him. True, he had urged them to hurry, but he'd never envisioned this.

The orb twisted and thrashed. Up and down, side to side, upside down, and right-side up. He hoped the ride ended soon. The last thing he wanted to do was hurl up his lunch inside a confined space that shifted positions.

Ajax didn't move when the orb landed on the beach. Nausea overwhelmed him and he needed a minute or two before he thought he could even attempt to stand up.

Giant silvery fish flopped onto the sand, shaking off all the water on them and shifting back into their human-like counterparts.

Ajax didn't want to be the last one ready so he unfastened the straps and rose, leaning on the stool for support. He staggered out of the orb and leaned back against it.

"I didn't know humans could change color. Green doesn't suit you," Bolin said, eyeing Ajax up and down.

He pushed himself off the globe and forced himself to stand upright. "I'm fine. Let's get going." The last thing he wanted to do was look weak in front of the mermen.

The portal swirled in front of them, hovering just above the sandy beach. Ajax double checked his bag, ensuring he still had the much-needed Mer flower, then removed the shell from his bag. It emitted a low glow.

He glanced up, noticing Bolin and the others had done the same. Then before Ajax could warn them about the blood-sucking bats, Bolin stepped through the portal, his soldiers following after him.

Ajax unsheathed his sword and rushed in after them, hoping these shells didn't attract the vampire bats.

Once through the portal, Ajax could see the immediate area around him. He held his sword at the ready and twirled around listening for sounds of incoming trouble. But silence greeted him.

"I'm not certain which way we need to go," Ajax said when he felt certain the bats weren't going to attack.

"You said we needed to head to the chasm, correct?" Bolin asked.

"Yes, but when the queen and I passed through this forest we didn't have these shells. Complete and utter darkness surrounded us. I have no idea which way we came."

"Perhaps if we just follow the signs," Bolin said, gesturing to a piece of wood hammered into a tree.

Ajax approached it and noticed markings etched into it with arrows pointing different directions. He couldn't make any sense of the writing.

He turned and surveyed the forest and for the first time, he noticed paths and other signs. The brief time he had light here, running for his life had been the priority. Ajax never noticed the order inside the forest.

"You can read this?" Ajax asked.

"Of course," Bolin said. "These were made by my people. If the elves had not become so bloodthirsty, we would have continued to come here. There is much we miss from the days of free trade throughout the realms."

"Magnificent. Lead the way," Ajax said.

It surprised Ajax that a journey through the forest of Never Ending Night could be so pleasant. The paths had become overgrown with the lack of travelers, but still evident. And with the light of the shells, the difficulty of traversing through the forest lessened. It almost felt enjoyable. Perhaps it would have been, if Ajax didn't carry the weight of what could happen to Nivara, or the uncertainty of the fates of Sky, Blake, and Leif.

The journey took almost no time at all. With no darkness to hinder them and signs marking the direction of the various landmarks, they reached the chasm just before nightfall.

"We will have to make camp here. The bridge to cross over will appear in the morning. Hopefully my friends are already in one of the towers. We don't have much time left."

The soldiers made a small fire and laid their blankets out as far from the edge of the cliffs as possible. One of the soldiers, a taller merman named Glendry, made a fish stew for their supper.

Ajax ate quickly and retired to his blanket, wrapping his

cloak around him to stay warm from the chill in the night air. His injuries continued to heal faster than he thought possible with the care of the mermaids, but his body still ached and didn't feel one hundred percent yet.

Tomorrow would be a long day. He'd need all his strength to face Striker. A plan wouldn't hurt either, but as much as he'd racked his brain, he just didn't see any way out of this.

Ajax had just closed his eyes when he heard the flapping of wings overhead.

"Elves!" he yelled, jumping up and searching for his sword in the dim light.

CHAPTER XXVI

Blake

By the time Blake landed beside the other winged creatures who had ventured through the portal with him, the elves had them all surrounded, each one armed and looking deadly.

Now this is what I expect from elves, Blake thought.

He slid down from the Jeda's back and made his way towards the front of the group.

By the time he reached the front, Nalva and Leif had pushed their way through the elves, insisting that they lower their weapons.

"Nalva, they've brought an army. Everything Lord Striker has told us about the other realms is true. Can't you see that?" one of the elves demanded, waving his arms towards Blake and his companions. "They've come to attack us just like the merpeople did years ago."

"I see them, Paxum," Nalva said. "Let's hear what they have to say."

"What army?" Sky asked looking around. "Do you see any weapons? These animals have come to offer you safe passage to Elf City. Step outside of these bogs and see the world as it truly is, not as some lies Striker has fed you."

"You speak treason," Paxum said, pointing a spear at Sky's throat.

Sky froze as the tip touched his fur.

"Enough!" Nalva exclaimed.

Paxum stepped back but did not lower his spear.

"They want us to ride them so they can soar up into the clouds. Then when they are high enough, they'll drop us to our deaths. It's a trick," Paxum said.

The elves gasped in horror at the idea.

"That is not true," Leif said. "I am one of you. Come with me, Mother, and see the truth for yourself."

"I am charged with protecting our people. Our children," Nalva said. "I cannot abandon them."

"Bring them with us. Even Striker would not harm them if you are present."

"They are not ready to leave," Nalva said. "I understand things are not as they seem. Your father has misled us. But there must be a reason. Go ahead of me. Give me time to convince our people to leave here."

"I have to go. Nivara does not have much time left. But Mother, please know this, if something happens to me, Striker did it. He wants me dead."

"Of everything you've told me, I still can't believe that to be true. But go now, and I will see you soon," Nalva said

She pulled Leif in for an embrace and kissed him softly on his cheek.

Leif turned to his friends. "Did you succeed in your quest?"

"When have I ever failed you?" Sky asked, cocking a bushy eyebrow up.

"Never," the elf smiled. "I wish I had succeeded in convincing my own people of Striker's lies."

"We will just have to prevail without them," Blake said.

"Jeda, will the rest of your friends stay here for a day or two in case the elves change their mind and want to leave?" Sky asked.

"If the elves stop pointing weapons at them, I think I can persuade them," Jeda said, moving into the crowd.

Leif turned to his mother, who nodded. She spoke something in Paxum's ear too quiet to be heard, but he lowered his weapons and turned, heading back to the village. As he did the others followed suit.

Nalva gave Leif one last nod as a farewell and retreated down the hill.

Jeda returned with his sister Mila at his side.

"They will stay until the day after tomorrow. Then, if the elves haven't changed their minds, they will return home," Jeda said.

"Thanks," Blake said. "Let's hope Nalva can convince them and herself."

It was a huge disappointment returning and not having these elves on their side. Blake had felt certain that Leif would be able to convince them. Showing the elven city that they had mothers, maybe even siblings like Leif, could have changed everything. Even Striker couldn't fight everyone. If they could have turned his people against him, they'd never have to risk giving him the elixir of immortality.

"We'd better get going. It will be dark soon and we need to meet Ajax and Neely at the tower," Sky said, looking up at the light that had already begun to fade..

"At least we won't run into any bog monsters this time," Leif said, sharing an uneasy look with Blake.

"We will take you to the tower and stay with you for as long as you need us," Mila said, lowering her wing and kneeling down.

"Thank you. I am Leif," the elf said as he climbed on.

"I'm Mila."

Sky jumped up beside Leif as Blake mounted Jeda. The two griffins flapped their wings and ascended into the darkening sky. Leif motioned the direction the griffins should fly and they shot off towards the tower.

Blake watched as the world below blurred past them. It still amazed him how much faster they could traverse the world flying versus riding a horse. But with no obstacles in their way they soared over the bogs in less than a half hour and landed in the courtyard of a tower, just as the last of the light faded into darkness.

"Ajax!" Sky called, leaping from Mila's back. "Neely!"

He scurried inside, then returned before Blake could do

more than dismount Jeda.

"They are not here," Sky said, his face full of disappointment.

"Maybe they are stuck on the cliffs," Leif suggested. "The bridge is only accessible in the morning, and as far as we know there are no flying creatures in the Mer Realm."

"Right," Sky said, scrambling up the railing around the tower.

Blake and Leif followed behind him.

"Look," Sky said. "You were right. I see a fire going."

"Good, they've made it back," Blake said, feeling relieved. "That means we can make the potion tonight and bring it to Striker in the morning."

"What if they couldn't find the flower?" Leif asked.

"Ajax found it. He wouldn't have returned without it. At least not until the last possible moment," Blake said.

"I'll go get them," Sky volunteered. "If Mila and Jeda don't mind another flight."

"It's not a long one," Mila said. "I can do it."

"Me too," Jeda said.

"Excellent," Sky said, bounding onto Jeda's back.

Blake watched as the griffins flew towards the campfire. Just one more day. One more day and Niv would be safe. Striker would be invincible, but at least Nivara would still be alive. They'd just have to find some dark pit to lock Striker in for the rest of eternity.

Even though Blake wanted to believe it would be that easy, he couldn't shake the sense of dread that clung to him. When had they ever bested Striker? Like a cockroach, he kept coming back, each time multiplying and bringing more of his kind.

But for now, he'd focus on saving Niv and then they'd figure out the rest, once he held her in his arms again.

Chapter XXVII

Nivara

The ground shaking beneath Niv woke her from her sleep. She stood up, brushing her clothes off and pulling straw out of her hair. It felt too early for breakfast. Exhaustion still filled her bones, so she didn't think she'd been asleep long.

The large door to her cell creaked as the troll pulled it open.

"Stepin," Niv said, startled at the sight of him. "You're okay. I thought that you'd been punished for showing kindness to me. I'm glad to see you're all right."

He held his finger to his lips and shushed her.

"It's time," he whispered.

Time for what? Niv wondered, hoping Striker had not summoned her.

"Put on the cloak and keep the cowl pulled down as much as you can."

It made sense now. Stepin was the mutual friend. Telkin sent him to assist her in escape.

Niv hurried to fasten the cloak, tucking her hair back and pulling the hood down to cover her face.

"Let's go," Stepin said. "Follow my lead and don't say a word to anyone."

The dungeon felt too quiet and Niv hesitated.

"Come on, we've no time to lose," Stepin said, reaching forward and tugging on the front of her cloak.

"Death will be the least of your worries if Striker catches us. Do you have any idea what you are risking?"

"I've been here a long time. I know Lord Striker. I've also known Leif. We played together some when we were younger. I'm not the only one who has noticed your loyalty and friendship to him. There is a change shifting in some of my kind. We don't see evil creatures out to destroy us when we look at humans, mermaids, and other creatures. You travel with friends from diverse backgrounds. You've earned their friendship and trust. We know what Lord Striker has demanded for your return. This isn't a charade. You have friends risking their lives for you. That is true friendship." He paused, looking at Niv with admiration. "We want to have that. Friendship and peace. Not all of us are war hungry. We follow Lord Striker because we fear to oppose him. At one time we thought he acted for the benefit of us. But we are seeing that he's misled us. Lied to us. We are the only species acting and inciting war. I will risk anything to see things change."

Niv nodded, wondering if what Stepin said could be true. Not that she thought he lied, but maybe it was wishful thinking. Could there be more than a few elves that felt like Leif, Stepin, and Telkin?

This time when Stepin led the way, Niv followed after him.

She kept her eyes down, helping the cowl to conceal her face more. The soldiers sent the troll back and appeared to not notice Niv and Stepin as they strolled past. Could they be sympathizers as well?

They reached the staircase that led out of the dungeons and Stepin took a torch off the wall. They made their way up the twisting staircase.

Niv's legs ached. She wondered how many times the soldiers went up and down these steps on a daily basis. Ascending the stairs took a lot more effort than descending.

By the time they reached the top, Niv grabbed Stepin by the shoulder and leaned against the wall.

"I need a minute," Niv panted.

Stepin nodded, dousing the torch in a bucket of water and leaning into the shadows with her. Niv could hear marching on the other side of the wall from where they stood.

After a moment she nodded and straightened herself.

"Many soldiers are being moved to guard the perimeter of the city and castle. We will blend in with them," he whispered before pushing open a door and falling in with rows and rows of soldiers filing through the castle.

Niv moved behind Stepin and followed him. It took her a second to get into the rhythmic march of the army. Hundreds of soldiers marched through the castle. Niv would need to pay sharp attention to the elf in front of her. If he turned or changed direction and she lost sight of him for a second, it would be impossible to find Stepin again.

They marched through corridor after corridor until Niv recognized the room they entered, Lord Striker's throne room.

It looked like Striker would be speaking a few inspired words to his troops before he sent them off. Niv kept her eyes to the ground and tried to focus on keeping pace and blending in. If she moved faster or slower than the other elves, it might catch his attention.

Striker stood at the top the stairs in front of his throne. He looked quite regal, though Niv hated to admit it.

He wore black trousers tucked into shiny black military boots. He had a fitted black tunic with a red vest and a red cape that hung down to the top of his boots.

Once all the elves had filed into the throne room, Striker cleared his throat and the room fell into silence.

"Tonight we prepare for a change that will turn the tide of this war. Be prepared for any surprises the sorcerer and his cohorts might try to spring on us. But know this, no matter what they do, we will be victorious. I hold the key to our success locked away in the dungeons. After tonight none shall ever be able to hurt me. Once we have verified the validity of the elixir, I shall scour the realms and replicate the tonic, until no elf anywhere shall ever have to fear these inferior creatures, who, despite their various attempts, have been unable to wipe us out. We shall finally be safe. All will fear us."

A cheer went up from the soldiers. Niv glanced around

nervously. They could not let Striker replicate the elixir. Fighting one crazed immortal elf that could not be killed would be hard enough; an entire army would be impossible.

Niv had to stop Ajax from giving it to Striker. If he couldn't test it, then Striker could still be stopped.

Once the cheering subsided, Striker continued.

"On to your posts. Tomorrow, we taste victory. Long live the elves!"

"Long live the elves!" the soldiers chanted.

"Long live the elves!"

The elves repeated the chant over and over again as they exited the throne room.

Stepin and Niv followed the soldiers as they filed out of the throne room and stepped into the corridor.

But before Niv could breathe a sigh of relief, a rough hand grabbed her.

"Not so fast," the voice said, dragging her back inside as soldiers filed past.

Niv looked around, hoping Stepin had escaped, but her heart plummeted as she saw another guard had him, a blade against his throat.

"Did you think I'd let you leave?" Striker asked. "And miss all the fun?" He laughed before motioning to another guard who stood in the far corner of the room. "I have eyes everywhere. After the failure of my firstborn, do you think I wouldn't keep a close watch on his sibling?" He shook his head and sighed. "This one turned out more disappointing than the first." He motioned to a soldier at his side.

The guard opened the door and several more soldiers filed in, pushing a bound and bloody creature towards the center of the room. The figure stumbled and tripped as the guards prodded it forward.

"Telkin!" Niv gasped.

He looked almost unrecognizable, his face bloody and swollen.

"How can you treat your own blood like this?" Niv said, then peered at the soldiers. "What do you think he'll do to you if he treats his own family this way?"

"What power do you have over my sons?" Striker scoffed. "Perhaps I have been a fool. Thinking all this time that women are the weaker sex. Maybe I should have brought one of my daughters here to fight at my side. Surely you would not have been able to bewitch her."

"Leave him alone," Niv said. "And Stepin, too. I'm the one you want. You have me, release them."

"Oh, how I am going to enjoy taking my time with you after this is over," he said, nodding to the guard that held Stepin.

Niv turned and felt relieved as the guard lowered the knife, but the relief turned to horror in a flash as the guard beat Stepin.

"Stop!" Niv cried.

"Oh, I won't kill him, either of them. At least not until they watch what I have in store for you. Think of it as a mercy." Striker smiled, showing far too many teeth. "I'm not going to make you watch as I kill them. I'm even going to wait for Leif, have a little family reunion before I end the male half of my line. After all, I won't need anyone to carry on after me. Once I'm invincible, I'll be here forever."

"You're a disgusting monster. Ajax will find a way to destroy you," Niv said, wiping the tears from her eyes.

"Enough," Striker said, raising his hand. The guard stopped hitting Stepin, who lay still on the floor.

Niv ran to him. Striker didn't stop her. She sobbed as she saw his unmoving face. She carefully wiped the blood off his face with the edge of her cloak and felt his breathing.

He still lived…for now.

"Ajax will do everything I intend him to do. In fact, he's on his way back here now. I have eyes watching him. I knew the first second he came through the portal, and I will know it when he enters my city. There is nothing that boy can do that I won't anticipate."

Three wooden contraptions rolled into the room, each pushed by two elves.

"Chain them up, then push them in front of my throne. In case I need some extra incentive for the boy."

A guard ripped Niv away from Stepin as another one shackled the Stepin's limp body by his feet and hung him over a platform of razor-sharp spikes. One slice through the rope holding him would mean the end of Stepin.

She tried to fight back but a second guard came, each one grabbing one of her arms and holding them back. In a few minutes they had tied Niv to a flat table, stretching her limbs out in the form of an X. Niv saw hand cranks at each corner of the table and hoped that her guess of their function was wrong.

Telkin groaned as two guards put him in a pillory, but slumped down, exhausted, once fastened in. Niv craned her neck to watch, trying to think of some way she could help him. To her horror she noticed that this particular pillory had been made with alterations, or at least altered from the pillories she had seen her realm.

Two long wooden beams jutted up several feet from the sides, connected at the top by a crossbeam. Under the beam hung a large shining blade attached to a rope on a pulley that had been tied off onto a post that stuck out from the bottom of the pillory, like a guillotine.

How would Ajax be able to save all of them?

CHAPTER XXVIII

Ajax

After a moment of frantic searching, Ajax's fingers curled around the hilt of his sword, bringing with it a small sense of control.

Bolin and the other mermen stood armed with bows, spears, and swords. The bowmen nocked their arrows and took aim at the flying beasts.

"Should we attack?" Bolin asked, waiting for Ajax to give the order.

"No, you shouldn't attack. I'm not a filthy elf," a voice shouted from above.

Despite the darkness of the night, Ajax would know that voice anywhere. A smile spread across his face and a sense of relief flooded through him. He lowered his own sword.

"Stand down," Ajax ordered, waving his hand at them to lower their weapons. "I was wrong, it's not the elves. These are our allies."

The griffins slowly circled downward, landing in the center of the small clearing. Sky bounded down from one of the animals' backs.

"I better be a little more than just an ally," Sky said, sounding wounded.

"You are to me, of course." Ajax laughed. "But the merpeople don't know you like I do. It's so wonderful to see you again. At times I didn't think I would." He knelt down and ruffled Sky's fur.

"Where's Neely? Did something happen to her?" Sky asked, noting her absence.

"Something, yes. Something bad…well we shall have to wait and see."

The mersoldiers stiffened and looked at Ajax with uncertainty.

"What do you mean?" Sky asked, his tone full of concern.

"She's queen of the mermaids. She stayed behind to…well, it's a little complicated, but she is unharmed," Ajax said.

"Neely is queen?"

A few of the mermen touched their weapons.

Ajax waved them off. "They prefer for you to refer to her as Her Highness or Her Majesty," Ajax said in a low voice.

Sky looked around at the armed men and nodded.

"So, you got the flower?" Sky asked, turning to business.

"Yes, and the hair?" Ajax asked.

"Plucked straight from a unicorn's tail." Sky smiled. "Now let's get back. I'm starving and we have a potion to make."

"Sky, Jeda is new to this body and his wings haven't built up a lot of strength. I don't think we can ferry everyone back tonight," the griffin with the violet eyes said, noting how many companions accompanied Ajax. "You had mentioned two and there are quite a few more."

"Bolin, I need to go over. Would your men be opposed to spending the night here? I can go by myself or you can come with me. We can reunite in the morning," Ajax said.

"I am to keep you safe. I made that vow to the queen before we departed. My men will stay here. We will go together."

Ajax nodded. He climbed onto the griffin that Sky had ridden over on, grabbing a tuft of fur to hold on to.

"I'm Ajax. Thank you for the ride," he said after he had mounted the beast.

"Mila, and that is my brother Jeda," she said.

"That's Bolin," Ajax said as the merman climbed onto Jeda's back. "So you both are cambriars, too."

"You are clever, I didn't think anyone would pick up on that," Mila said as she took to the skies.

"I've been around this one for quite a while," Ajax said as he stroked Sky. The hoosula arched his back and leaned towards Ajax, encouraging him to continue.

"Yeah, he's all right," Sky said, grinning.

A large fire roared in the middle of the courtyard. The smell of roasted pheasant floated up on the breeze. Ajax noted Leif turning the spit as Blake piled more wood onto the fire.

Mila landed gracefully on the stone floor while Jeda landed with a large thud.

"Let's eat," Sky said, hurrying over to the others.

"You eat, I've had dinner," Ajax said. "I want to get started on the elixir. It will take some time to prepare. Bolin, you're welcome to assist me or eat with Sky."

Bolin rubbed his chin in thought. "I think I'd like to try some of the food humans eat. I can watch you from the fire."

"It's delicious," Sky said.

Blake waved a greeting to Ajax before turning to fetch his bag, then brought it over to where Ajax stood.

"Let's get started," Blake said.

Ajax dug in his bag and took out the parchment with the notes he had written on it.

"We need a couple of vials. Something we can seal off with wax to keep the liquid secure until we meet up with Lord Striker."

"I'll find something inside," Blake said, pointing to a large pot on the ground. "I thought we could use that to make it."

"That ought to work," Ajax said.

The prince turned and disappeared into the tower as Ajax unrolled the parchment.

Tin kuid vinkuro hors isto sol dur

Ajax reread the words. If only they made sense.

"Twenty-four hours," Mila said, leaning over Ajax's shoulders. "What's the rest say?"

"You can read some of this?" Ajax asked.

"Not all of it. I never paid much attention to the ancient languages of our world. I learned the numbers and time and slept through the rest of the lessons. It says something, then twenty-four hours, and then something else I can't decipher."

"Did Jeda learn this too?" Ajax asked, looking at the other griffin who tore open a pheasant with a large talon, then tore a big hunk of meat off.

Mila laughed loudly. "Of the two of us, I was ten times more studious than him. I think he slept through ninety percent of the lessons."

"Well, it's worth a try," Ajax said. He picked up the parchment and brought it over to Jeda. But Mila had been telling the truth. Jeda could make out less of the language than his sister.

"My apologies, I wish I could offer you more assistance," he said before turning back to his meal.

Ajax stared at the words. Twenty-four hours. Twenty-four. The note didn't have to do with the brewing of the potion. The instructions for that had been written in extraordinary detail.

So why the note?

A crazy idea struck Ajax. Could it be wishful thinking? Perhaps. Regardless, he decided not to share it. Either he'd be right or wrong. No sense in getting the others' hopes up if the latter ended up being true.

Blake returned and together they prepared the potion. The

ingredients being scarce and with no way to replace them, they worked slowly. First Ajax and then Blake would read the instructions, then they discussed each step before attempting it. The dragon shells needed to be crushed while the directions for the magical glowing flower said to dice it. Both of these needed to be mixed in water and simmered for three hours before dropping the unicorn hair into the mixture and removing it at once from heat.

They collected sufficient ingredients to prepare the elixir twice.

The first time Ajax did all the mixing and chopping, and the second time Blake took a turn preparing it. By morning the boys had just finished sealing the bottles with melted wax stoppers.

As the morning light began to push the darkness from the night away, Ajax stood and stretched his arms and legs. It still baffled him that they could have night and day without a sun.

"I guess we won't be getting any sleep," Ajax noted, looking at the sky.

"We can sleep once we have Nivara back safe and sound," Blake said.

"Did you succeed in making the potion?" Bolin asked, walking over to them.

"Time will tell. Now we should probably come up with some sort of rough plan," Ajax said.

"Plan?" Leif asked as he sat up from his blanket. "You have

a plan for defeating Striker? Let's hear it."

"Defeat Striker?" Sky said, yawning. "I'd like to hear how we plan on pulling that one off."

Ajax ran a hand through his hair. "I said we should come up with one, not that I had one."

"You distract Striker, the rest of us rescue Niv. Simple strategies are the best," Blake said.

"Easy as that?" Leif asked, shaking his head.

"It won't be easy but we have to succeed. I don't care it what it takes. We save Niv. Sky, you get her out of there no matter what. Even if it means leaving the rest of us behind," Blake said.

"Agreed," Leif said, nodding.

"Striker will have her under heavy guard, or in some dangerous predicament," Ajax said. "I'll do my best to assist in rescuing her, but I don't have my medallion. I'll be vulnerable."

"Leif, you protect Ajax. We shall need his magic. Sky and I will rescue Niv," Blake said.

"We can help," Mila said.

"I also came with several mermen skilled at fighting to offer Ajax our assistance. But how will we all get there?" Bolin asked.

"Mila, getting us to the elven city will be a tremendous help," Blake said. "After that it would be best if you get out of sight. We will need to get Niv away as fast as we can. Watch for us and if you see any of us emerge with a girl, come fetch us."

Then he turned to Bolin. "We have to get there today or they will kill Nivara. Mila and Jeda can't carry all of us. We can give you a map to get the elven city. The journey will be longer but you may still be able to help us. We have no idea what lies in store for us."

"I promised Her Majesty that I would protect you. But I can't leave all my men behind in this new world," Bolin said, looking torn.

"She will understand and so do I. This is our best option for now. You should hurry though. The bridge is only accessible in the early morning. Return to your men now."

Bolin nodded, and Sky volunteered to show him the bridge.

Then Ajax turned to Leif. "Take one of these," he said, passing a vial to Leif. "Striker wants this more than anything. I don't want to risk them clashing together in my pocket and breaking. I feel better knowing there is a backup."

Leif took the vial and looked at it. The blueish liquid sloshed inside. "I cannot believe this little vial can hold so much power."

"If we made it right," Ajax said, shrugging. "First time trying to make a magic potion."

"If we are lucky, it will poison him," Leif said.

"Then it would poison one of us, too," Blake said. "If you are correct and Striker makes someone try it first."

"I would be happy to die if it means the end of Striker," Leif said, tucking the vial into a pocket in his cloak.

"Let's hope it doesn't come to that," Ajax said.

"Enough of this morbid talk. Let's eat and then go save Niv," Sky said, returning to them after Bolin departed.

They ate a quick meal of eggs and bread. Then Ajax rose and looked at the two griffins. He wondered if they'd be able to carry two full sized men. Their size didn't compare to that of a dragon, and Sliver never liked to carry more than two passengers.

"Do you think one of you can handle carrying two of us?" Ajax asked.

"How far do we need to fly?" Mila asked, looking at Jeda.

Her brother still looked tuckered out from the flights yesterday. Ajax had never been to Elf City and had no idea of the distance so he deferred to Leif.

"A fair distance," the elf answered. "I am not sure of the difference between flying on a griffin versus a langabeast. But it would take a good two hours on a langabeast."

"Two hours," Jeda repeated, shaking his head. "I'm not sure I can make it that far with one, let alone two. Muscles ache that I didn't even know I had."

"We will do our best," Mila said. "I'll take two and my brother can take Sky and the other. I'm not used to carrying passengers but I've been in this body for almost a month now. My wings are strong, and my endurance is built up. I have the best chance of carrying more weight."

"Okay, Ajax and I will ride on Mila, and Leif, you and Sky ride on Jeda. That way if anything happens, one rider will still have an elixir," Blake said.

Leif nodded.

"So this is it. The big battalion to fight Striker," Ajax said, wishing they had a bigger group.

"It's the keeper's battalion. How can we go wrong?" Blake said.

"Why mine?" Ajax said, sounding surprised.

The prince put a hand on Ajax's shoulder. "Because we wouldn't be here without you. You came after me through the portal. You defeated the elves on top of this very courtyard. You saved my parents from the elves. And you helped me keep my head after Nivara was taken." He paused. "I know we haven't always seen eye to eye, but I know we never would have gotten this far without you."

Ajax stood speechless, unsure of how to respond.

"If I had to pick a team, it would be you three," Sky said, trying to echo the sentiment. "Sliver would be nice too. And I wouldn't oppose Niko and that sharp ax he totes around...and maybe—"

"Okay I think we get the point. Now let us go save Nivara," Leif said.

Ajax let Blake climb up first and pulled himself up behind him. He felt nervous. What if they couldn't save Nivara?

As they took flight Ajax reached out to her. He hadn't tried to contact Nivara since he first arrived. He had assumed the connection wouldn't reach the Mer Realm since he couldn't connect with her from Rastella.

Niv, he thought.

Ajax, don't come.

He didn't know how to explain it, but her thought sounded tired and weak.

Niv, we are coming for you. Hold on. He sent the second thought.

Danger, new friends in trouble.

Did Striker already know about the griffins assisting him? Could their lives be in danger?

Niv, what do you mean? he asked.

No answer came.

Niv?

His stomach churned with worry at Nivara's lack of response. He hoped she had fallen asleep but thoughts of what Striker could be doing to her flooded his mind.

The griffins flew high where the wind blew harder, using the strong breezes to help them fly with less effort. They flew over the desert.

Blake had told Ajax stories of the intense heat he faced when he had fallen into this desert after entering the portal. Ajax felt grateful he now flew across it and did not have to travel by foot. Whether from the breezes or the fact that they flew so high, the heat didn't reach them now.

Soon they flew across a large jungle. Trees stretched out for miles. Vines with colorful flowers intertwined between the plant life. Ajax noticed some small ponds scattered throughout the jungle as well as a long river that ran east to west.

He glanced over at Leif and Sky riding on the blue-eyed Jeda. They appeared deep in conversation. From where Ajax sat it looked a little heated, but from what he had no clue.

"After this you should think about learning how to create your own portals. How much easier would it be to escape if you had that feather in your cap," Blake said, then pointed forward. "Because I don't know how we will be able to leave once we get inside."

Ajax shifted his gaze in Blake's direction. The elven city came into view and with it an astonishing sight. The city itself lay surrounded by an army of at least a dozen deep, encircling the entire city. And then further in, at what had to be the castle where Striker dwelled, another group of soldiers stood guarding. Everywhere Ajax looked an armed elf, or twenty, waited. He couldn't even venture a guess as to how many elves Striker commanded.

"We have to kill him," Ajax said. "Striker," he added, as if he needed to clarify. "That may be the one chance we have. A new leader will emerge, perhaps even Leif. Someone we can reason with."

"Did you see what the elves did to Rastella?" Blake asked,

shaking his head. "There is no reasoning with them. I think this is a mission we will not return from." He placed his hand on Ajax's shoulder. "At least Niv will know we tried. We didn't abandon her. Thank you."

Ajax didn't know how to respond. He saw no way out of this, but he would not give up hope. People he loved waited for him back in Rastella. Neely, the new queen of the merpeople, had faith in him. He would not leave them to fight an invincible Striker on their own.

He had one card left to play and he prayed that it worked.

"Mila, set us down over there in that clearing," Ajax said, motioning toward an area in front of the city gates.

"Are you crazy?" Blake asked.

"Striker still needs us. We can't sneak in. Look at all those soldiers. That meadow is far enough away that Jeda and Mila should be able to take off again without us worrying what the soldiers will do, and close enough that the army will know that we are not afraid. We are not trying to sneak in. We are going in through the front gate."

Blake looked at Ajax with uncertainty but finally shrugged.

"I hope you know what you are doing," he said.

"Me too," Ajax said under his breath.

Mila and Jeda landed in the clearing but hesitated before taking off again.

"Are you certain you want to face that?" Jeda asked, swinging his long tail in the direction of the soldiers. "I'm exhausted but I could fly us out of sight and then we could rest before going home."

"We can't," Sky said. "Would you leave Mila in there?"

Jeda twisted his large eagle head almost upside down and looked at his sister as if contemplating the answer to the question. Then he straightened his head and turned back.

"I suppose not," he said.

"Ha ha," Mila said, "We will keep our promise. Stay out of sight and come for you should we see you emerge. Best of luck. You are braver than me. Or maybe just crazier."

Ajax could read the skepticism on her face and couldn't blame her. The more he thought about what they faced the more doubts he too had.

"Thank you. We appreciate your willingness to get involved and not just sit back and let evil prevail," Ajax said. "We never would have made it here on time without you." He looked to Leif and Sky, then finally to Blake.

"After you," Blake said.

"You're too kind, Your Highness," Ajax said, and winked at him. He strode forward, holding his head high. If Striker watched them from some high tower in his kingdom, Ajax didn't want him to see any fear.

As they reached the first of the soldiers standing in front of the city gate, a soldier with a red sash stepped forward.

Presumably he carried more authority over the other elves.

"Leave your weapons and I will escort you to see Lord

Striker," the soldier ordered.

The others looked to Ajax, waiting to follow his lead.

"I don't think so," Ajax said. "We don't trust Striker. I have brought what he demanded, but we will ensure he keeps his side of the bargain."

Ajax noticed Blake moving a hand in a casual manner towards the hilt of his sword, while Leif stretched his arm, close to the arrows in his quiver.

"There are more of us than there are of you," the soldier said, peering back behind him.

"I am pretty certain Striker wouldn't want anything to happen to this," Ajax said, pulling out a vial with bright blue liquid. "So, step aside or I shall move you." He slid the vial in his cloak and placed his hand over the ground using his magic to make it shake.

"All right, stop," the soldier said, having a challenging time maintaining his balance.

Ajax lowered his hand and the ground stilled. Then the soldier leaned forward, getting a little too close for Ajax's comfort, and whispered in his ear. "When you leave, the same rules don't apply. Or should I say if you leave." He sneered at Ajax as he stepped back and motioned for the men to step aside and open the gate.

"That went easier than I'd have thought," Sky said, jumping from Leif to Ajax's shoulder.

"He wants us to reach him. I am not certain what he has in

store once we find him. Whatever it is, we shall probably regret reaching him," Leif said.

"Traitor."

"Traitor."

"Traitor."

Ajax could hear the words, some whispered, some said with contempt and spite as they made their way through the city. He wondered if it bothered Leif at all or if he'd given up any thought of ever being a part of his people.

There had been no time to swap stories on their recent adventures. Blake and Leif looked banged up, so he knew their journey hadn't been smooth. He wondered if they found the elf mothers. If they survived this, they'd have the rest of their days to share stories.

The city itself stood deserted. Every elf must have been on the perimeter of the city or at the castle itself. Ajax kept his eyes on the buildings just in case. Striker liked to surprise them. He noticed his companions doing the same.

As they continued along, Ajax noticed a lone soldier hiding in the shadows between two buildings. Leif stood closest and Ajax motioned with his eyes to Leif.

He nocked an arrow and made his way to the alley.

Ajax could see them conversing before Leif let him go and fell back in step with the others.

"He didn't try to kill you?" Blake asked.

"No," Leif said, looking perplexed. "He said he is a friend

to my brother, Telkin. He said Telkin tried to save the girl and that Striker is going to kill him."

"Do you believe him?" Ajax asked.

"It could be a trap," Sky said. "In fact, I bet it's the most likely option."

"I do not know. I have never seen much kindness among the elves. But my mother raised my brother. Something most elves do not experience. Also, I can see Nivara being able to convince others of the lies of my father. She exudes kindness and she draws people to her. So it may be possible. Either way, we need to stay alert," Leif said, continuing to watch the shadows.

Another soldier in a red sash stepped forward as they approached the steps that led into the castle.

"Leav—" the soldier began.

"Step aside or I shall move you," Ajax said, tired of the games. "I shall not ask again. Consider yourself warned."

"How dare you," the soldier said, but Ajax didn't wait for him to finish.

He put his hands together and then pulled them apart envisioning the elves making a path for him. As he did, his magic moved the elves to the sides as if shoved by an invisible wall.

They started forward and Ajax noticed a few elves reaching for their weapons. He met their gaze and stared at them with such an intensity they soon stopped and melted into the crowd.

“Now why can you not just fling all the elves inside against the walls, allowing us to grab Niv and get out of here?” Blake asked.

“Because my magic is not so precise. Striker always has a plan. He’ll be holding Niv at knife point, or he’ll have some other threat ready. If I try to fling the blade away, I’d be certain to cut Nivara as well. Striker knows enough about the power I hold to not do anything hasty. He’s had time to plan. More time than us. He planned this for months, before the invasion on Rastella. I bet his mind hasn’t stopped since I hurled the elves from the tower.”

“Yes, just do that again. He had a knife to Nivara then and you saved us all,” Blake said.

Ajax clasped Blake’s arm, turning the prince until they faced one another.

“I appreciate your faith in me, but I need you to listen. I don’t want you to have some misguided idea of what I am capable of. The tower was a fluke. I had the medallion which added to my power and Striker stood above Niv holding the knife, so when I flung it backwards, I had no chance of hitting her. Striker witnessed everything. He has been two steps ahead of us the entire time. When we find him, I will do what I can, but I am not the all-powerful Ajax Maxwell I may have acted like. Sliver saved Nivara. She would have died without him.”

“You’re wrong,” Blake said, shaking his head. “I was wrong too. Wrong to think you didn’t deserve these powers. I may have been a little bit jealous. You have been hasty and rash, but you needed time to develop this ability. Time I didn't always give you. But you are the all-powerful Ajax Maxwell. It just doesn't have to do completely with magic."

Blake pointed at his chest. "You're loyal, honorable, and a better friend I've never met. You'd do anything for those around you. Not to mention this works pretty good too." He tapped Ajax's skull. "When we survive this today, it will be because of you."

"Okay, enough of this mushy stuff. We have an evil elf lord to conquer," Sky said, bounding ahead.

Blake spun around and hurried after the others. Ajax stood for a moment, speechless, glad for Sky's interruption.

He looked over his shoulder one last time at the giant army gathered and rushed in after his friends

CHAPTER XXIX

Blake

The inside of the castle appeared deserted. It made for an uncomfortable feeling as they crept down passageways. The rhythmic thumping of Blake's heart sounded loud in his ears and he wondered if the others could hear it.

Nivara waited in one of these rooms for him. He had traveled to different realms, fought hideous creatures, and flown on the back of a griffin all to get to this moment. At times he didn't know if he'd survive. If he'd get to see her again. If he'd be able to tell her he loved her.

Fear filled him now, more with each step closer to seeing her. Not for what could happen to him, but for what Striker may have already done.

"Where should we look?" Blake whispered. He felt a little silly whispering when they appeared to be the only people in the castle, but it felt wrong to be any louder.

"The throne room. That is where I think he would position himself. Up high on the dais. Looking down on us," Leif said.

"That sounds about right to me," Ajax agreed.

"I hate that room," Sky said. "Nothing good ever happened in that room."

Blake didn't think he wanted to know what Sky referred to, so he refrained from asking any questions.

They followed Leif down the hallway until they reached a room where the doors stood open.

The glowing torches reflecting off the obsidian walls made the room feel ominous. Blake saw Nivara before he entered the room.

He dashed forward, running towards her.

"Halt!" a voice boomed. "Any closer and they die."

Blake skidded to a stop. Striker stood at the top of the stairs in front of the gaudiest throne he'd ever seen.

Ajax, Leif, and Sky stood beside him within moments.

An elf with dark hair had been locked inside a mechanism that looked like a new-fangled guillotine. A soldier positioned beside it held an ax high, ready to send the blade crashing down, which would in turn sever the neck.

Next to them, another contraption sat with Nivara chained to it. She had been pulled taut and looked in pain. Four soldiers manned the corners where a crank jutted out. If each elf simply applied a little pressure, Niv's agony would increase exponentially.

A third device had been rolled in. Large metal spikes shot up from the platform, and another elf hung, suspended by a rope above them.

But Blake didn't care about the other two prisoners. His sole focus lay with Nivara. He wondered for a brief moment if one of these men could be Leif's brother and the warning had been accurate, but he pushed the thought away. He couldn't afford to spend a moment worrying about them. At least not until he rescued Nivara.

"Did you bring what I wanted?" Striker asked, sitting down on his throne, looking as if he didn't have a care in the world.

Ajax stepped in front of the others and pulled out the vial, holding it up for Striker to see.

Blake looked around the room, scanning for all the possible exits and noticed soldiers lining the inside of the throne room.

"Now let her go," Ajax said.

"Foolish boy, I'm not doing anything until I see that the potion works. I hope that's not the only one you made. I'm not about to test something I haven't seen proof of with my own eyes."

Leif pulled the second vial out of his cloak. "We have two," he said.

"Well, if in fact they work, I'll have to search you all to ensure there aren't more duplicates. Now bring them both forward, sorcerer. And be warned: if you try anything, my soldiers know what to do."

What was Ajax's plan here? He couldn't just hand the elixir over without securing Nivara first.

"Not yet. How will you know if the potion works? Who will you test it on?" Ajax asked.

"That's an excellent question. One I've given considerable

thought to. I could give it to the girl, but then if it killed her, I'd lose my leverage. And if it worked, I'd still lose my leverage since I would be unable to inflict pain on her," Striker said, stroking his chin. "Then I thought perhaps my traitorous son should test it, but death by poison would be too merciful, and again if it worked, I wouldn't want to give him such a gift after his betrayal."

"The prince…well, he couldn't even keep his girl safe. So, I guess you will be the one to test the potion. After all, you've proved your obedience thus far by collecting all the ingredients and making the potion. And I know you value this girl's life." He glanced at her with a look of disdain. "Although I can't find anything remarkable about her. You've proven how much you value life. You could have saved this girl with your power but you won't risk the lives of these two insignificant elves you don't even know. I will even make you more powerful than me, giving you invincibility along with the magic you already possess. And when the other realms see how I've defeated you, all will know that I am unstoppable. Now bring me both," Striker demanded.

"No, you're not getting this until Niv is released. Pick a vial and I'll drink it. The one in my right hand or the one in my left. After you've tested it, then we can renegotiate," Ajax said.

"You're not as stupid as you look. But we both know I hold all the cards here. Now stop stalling and hand the one in your left hand back to Leif. I don't want you to try to switch vials on me after I've selected one."

Ajax did as instructed, trying to think of a way he could save all three lives at once.

"Now give the other vial to the prince. I forget his name, not that it matters," Striker said, waving a hand towards Blake.

Blake clasped the vial in a tight fist. If it slipped now there could be terrible consequences.

"Take the one from…" Striker looked back and forth between Blake and Leif. "…from Leif. I don't trust anything he has touched."

All eyes were glued on Ajax as he unstopped the vial and upended the contents in his throat. The taste must have been unpleasant. Ajax squeezed his eyes shut and grimaced as he swallowed.

"Now stab him straight through the heart," Striker said, motioning to a soldier positioned against the wall.

"No," Ajax said, holding up his hand, daring the soldier to come forward.

"I have to see if it works," Striker said. "That's the whole point of this entire exercise. Why drink it if you didn't intend to demonstrate its validity to me?"

"The recipe said it needs a few minutes to work," Ajax said.

Time ticked by slowly as they waited. It felt like agony to

Blake, seeing Niv in pain and not being able to do a thing to help her.

"That's it, I'm not waiting any longer," Striker said, motioning to the soldier.

Ajax took a knife from his boot and pricked his finger. Or tried to. Nothing happened.

"All right," Ajax said to the soldier who had taken a step forward but then hesitated. "Go ahead, do your worst."

The soldier drew closer and Ajax closed his eyes as the elf drew his sword.

Blake gripped the hilt of his on instinct and then released it. Ajax allowed this to happen, so Blake needed to trust him.

Holding the sword more like a dagger with both hands, the elf thrust the point downward. The force pushed Ajax backwards and he nearly fell from losing his balance, but he remained uninjured.

Blake wished he'd been ordered to take the potion. He'd be better able to protect Nivara if he couldn't get hurt.

"Now, give me the other vial," Striker said.

"Release the girl first," Ajax said.

"So you can then attack me?" Striker said, "I will release her after I have the vial. I'm not a fool. You're now invincible. I will not relinquish my leverage until the same can be said of me."

Blake watched as Ajax handed the vial to the soldier.

"What are you doing?" Blake asked.

"What choice do we have?" Ajax said.

"He is right, there are three lives at stake," Leif said.

"You mean seven," Sky said. "I mean, our lives count too."

Striker drank the vial in one greedy gulp, then waited for several minutes before testing his own dagger out on himself.

A horrid laugh escaped his lips when he found that the dagger would not pierce his skin.

"Now I will be unstoppable." He smiled wickedly. "And I've changed my mind. I don't think I will release the girl. She's been an awful lot of trouble but she has proven her usefulness when it comes to you. Besides, having a sorcerer in my pocket will be useful."

Blake looked at Ajax. His plan had failed. Now Striker couldn't be killed and he still had Niv.

"I won't be your pawn," Ajax said.

"You already are; you've done everything I've asked," Striker said.

"That was when I thought you'd keep your word. I won't let you torture Niv or use us. We'd all rather die, and while I might not be able to kill you, I'll bring this entire castle down on you and see how much your invincibility is worth with a thousand tons of stone on you."

"You wouldn't," Striker said.

"To keep the people of Rastella and the other realms safe, just watch me," Ajax said.

Blake watched Striker intently. He hesitated, thinking of what Ajax threatened.

"I'm going to have to call your bluff," Striker said, smiling smugly.

Ajax put up his hands and pulled at the walls and the ceilings. The entire room shook and dust and small chunks of mortar rained down. Sky hid between Leif's legs.

It took everything in Blake not to run straight to Nivara, to lay his body over hers and protect her from the rubble. But somehow, he managed to stop himself. Nivara trusted Ajax. So he would too.

Large cracks shot across the walls and ceiling as the shaking intensified.

"All right! Stop!" Striker said.

Ajax lowered his hands and the room fell into silence.

"I believe we are at a stalemate," Striker said. "If I release the girl, you could still collapse the room in on me as soon as you exit. If I keep the girl…well I get the picture. So, what do you suggest?" Striker asked.

"A duel," Ajax said.

"I cannot be killed or injured," Striker said, reminding Ajax of his recent transformation.

"The first to disarm the other," Ajax said.

"I will not fight you; I don't trust you to not use your magic," Striker said.

"I will not be the one fighting you. Prince Blake is more

skilled at sword fighting than me. If he disarms you, we leave and you surrender. If you win, we will surrender to you," Ajax said.

"What are you doing?" Blake asked, pulling on Ajax's sleeve.

"It is far easier to injure an opponent first and then disarm him. Striker will have all the advantage," Leif said.

"This is not your best plan," Sky agreed.

"I accept. We shall begin," Striker said, taking off his cape.

"No, give us twenty-four hours. We've had a few trying days; he deserves a good night's sleep and a proper meal. After all, Leif is right. You shall still have the advantage."

"Fine, but the girl will remain with me," Striker said, motioning for the soldiers to follow him out.

As the elves bent down and untied her, Niv gasped out in relief.

"If you hurt her, I will bring more than a throne room down on your head," Ajax vowed.

Striker nodded and exited the room with Nivara being carried by his side.

Leif ran forward, releasing the other two elves from their torture contraptions.

Ajax and Blake ran forward to help.

"Your father just left them here," Sky said.

"I think you surprised him for the first time and he lost his train of thought," Leif said.

"Do you think one of these is your brothers?" Sky asked.

"This is Stepin. I know him. But this other elf," Leif pointed to the dark-haired elf, "could be. He is new. I have never laid eyes on him before. I am going to go find some medical supplies. Do not let them be taken," Leif said.

"I'll come with you," Sky said.

When they had gone, Blake spun on Ajax.

"Are you crazy?" Blake asked.

"I just might be," Ajax said.

"This isn't a joke," Blake said, grasping Ajax's shirt. "Niv and all of our lives depend on it."

"Do you think I don't know that? It's the one chance we have," Ajax said. "Now do you want to stay angry or would you like to hear the rest of my plan?"

Sleep didn't find Blake that night. Too much depended on his skill with the sword. Everything hinged on Ajax's crazy plan that came from a hunch. Tomorrow Blake would either save the woman he loved or doom them all to painful deaths. If he had to die, he hoped he'd be executed first. He knew it to be a selfish thought, but he couldn't stand to watch Nivara die.

Ajax would keep his word and surrender if Striker won. Sometimes Blake wished he had a little less integrity, especially knowing their opponent had none.

CHAPTER XXX

Nivara

Niv drifted in and out of consciousness. It became hard to recognize reality from dream. Besides the pain she endured from being tied to a torture device, she felt like she'd been drugged. Striker gave her a few sips of water; he must have put something in it.

She had a vague memory of Ajax, Blake, Leif, and Sky arriving, but couldn't be certain that it hadn't been a dream.

Now at least her wrists and ankles remained unbound and she lay in a soft bed. Soldiers guarded the doorway. She tried to sit up but collapsed back onto the pillow and fell into a deep sleep.

Morning light shining down on Niv's face jarred her from her slumber. Her muscles ached and her wrists and ankles remained red and raw, but her head felt clear.

Ajax, Niv thought.

She didn't know what to hope for. A part of her wanted her friends to be here, to give her hope that rescue might be possible. But the other part of her knew that if they came and she hadn't dreamt it all then Striker could now not be hurt. And nothing terrified her more than the thought of that psychotic elf having more power.

Niv!

She felt pure joy through the expression of his thoughts.

Where are you? she thought back.

Here. In Striker's castle. With Blake, Sky, and Leif. They all miss you.

You need to leave me, Niv sent.

Don't worry. We have a plan. It's a little mad, but we are due a little bit of luck.

Promise me you won't save me if it risks the lives of our family. Stopping Striker is more important than saving me. Promise me, Niv pleaded in her mind.

I need to go. See you soon.

He could be so frustrating. He could pop into her head whenever he desired it, but she could only do it if he allowed it.

What plan could stop Striker? She'd seen the number of soldiers at his command.

It felt like hours passed before soldiers at last came to retrieve Nivara. She wondered if she'd see her friends now. Striker met her in the hallway, two soldiers flanking him. He'd changed his clothing and stood in all white—white boots, pants, and tunic.

The guards drew their swords when she stepped into the

hallway and pointed them at her as she walked, as if she had the energy to run.

"This is to ensure your friends keep their word," Striker said. "But they've made a foolish bargain and in a few minutes time we shall have that fun I've been promising you." His sneer made her shiver. "Or at least it will be fun for me."

The soldiers escorted her back into the throne room to a chair that had been placed next to the throne. Once she had taken a seat, the soldiers pointed their swords, one at her neck and one at her heart.

Her heart leapt at the sight of her friends. Blake stood with his back to her, whispering to Leif and Ajax. Sky waved up at her, and she smiled back despite her predicament.

Blake removed his cloak and withdrew his sword, giving it a few practice swings.

"Are you sure you want to take off Edwin's cloak?" Leif asked. "The dragon scales can offer you protection in the fight."

Blake shook his head. "I'm not practiced in fighting with a cloak. I think it would hinder my movements, putting me more at risk. I think fighting without it offers me a better chance than with it."

"Are you ready, boy?" Striker asked, swishing a sword of his own. "Remember, any interference and my soldiers will not hesitate."

"We keep our word," Blake said.

Niv couldn't believe it. Blake and Striker were about to fight. To what end? Striker couldn't be harmed, and Blake already had visible bruises.

Blake stepped forward and Striker advanced in a sudden attack. The prince parried his advances but received a small scratch on his left arm.

"This is going to be fun," Striker said. "In fact, I'm a little disappointed that I didn't come up with the idea."

Blake turned to the offensive with a mighty overhead strike. As Striker brought his sword up to block, Blake kicked him in the stomach. Striker stumbled back but kept his sword up.

"You do have some skill," Striker said as he feigned to the right, "but it won't be enough.

Blake didn't fall for his trick; he sidestepped around Striker, dropping his shoulder and slashing at his leg.

But nothing happened.

Niv noticed Blake looked to Ajax who waved him on to continue. Didn't they realize that Striker couldn't be hurt? What did they hope to accomplish from this duel, other than getting Blake killed?

Blade clashed against blade in quick succinct blows as they continued to fight. Striker drove Blake back and then the prince would change positions and drive Striker back.

Niv watched, her eyes glued to Blake. He fought with tremendous skill but eventually he'd tire and Striker just needed a lucky hit or two.

"Come on, Blake," Ajax shouted. "Now's the time."

Blake blocked another blow and sidestepped just in time to miss a second swing. Then he feigned an attack to the right, then the right again, and spun, slicing his sword across Striker's left leg.

"AHHH!"

Red bled through his white pants.

Niv couldn't believe her eyes.

"Impossible," Striker said, reaching down to touch his wound.

Blake took the chance to attack, one, two, three strong hits against Striker's sword and it went flying from his grasp. The point of Blake's sword rested against the elf's neck.

"But how?" Striker said, still not understanding what happened.

"It doesn't matter. It's over now. We are going to lock you up and throw away the key," Blake said. "That's the least you deserve after everything you've done."

"Release her," Ajax said as Leif bounded up the steps to Niv.

The soldiers dropped their swords and put their hands up.

"Where's the dungeon in this place?" Blake asked.

"Allow me," Leif said.

He hugged Niv, then hurried down towards Blake.

As Blake lowered his sword slightly, Striker grabbed Leif, pressing a dagger to his throat.

The knife must have been concealed in his waistband.

"You may have me, but at least I'll take him with me," Striker said.

Niv watched in horror. Blake raised his sword but looked to Ajax for advice.

"We can work something out," Ajax said.

"Say goodbye to your friends, son," Striker said as he pushed the point of the knife into his throat.

Blood trickled down Leif's neck.

"Release him now," a voice yelled from behind them.

Niv looked up to see a female elf striding forward, looking madder than a mother bear whose cubs were threatened.

Behind her, hundreds of animals, inflaters, merpeople, and other creatures filed in, armed and ready to fight.

Niv saw Niko with a group of rhinos.

To Nivara's astonishment, Striker loosened his grip of Leif.

"Nalva, what are you...This elf's a traitor..." Striker began to stutter.

"Release my son. I didn't believe him. I couldn't believe that you would harm our child, but I can't deny what my eyes now see," Nalva said.

"This isn't Telkin," Striker said.

"You have manipulated and lied to me too many times. I know my son. I have seen the marking. Release Leif this instant. Your army has surrendered. I've brought all the elves you've kept hidden away, and now everyone is seeing through your lies. How did you become this twisted monster?" She shuddered. "Lying to me. Depriving me of raising my child. Allowing me to mourn for him for all these years, letting a piece of me die?"

Striker let go of Leif and he ran forward and embraced his mother.

"How could you? You told me he died," Nalva said, her voice cracking.

"It was the only way. The council voted me off. They thought my ideas too radical. So I killed them. I knew I could bring our people to see their true potential, to rise to their rightful place as rulers over all the realms.

"I needed to convince everyone I was the right one to lead, so I burned the bodies. I blamed it on the merpeople but I didn't know if it would be enough. But the death of an innocent, now that would convince everyone. Once we had conquered the world, I would have brought you home, and found Leif being kept as a slave or prisoner in one of the realms. But he never embraced the true nature of his heritage. We deserve to rule. We are the superior species!"

Behind Nalva, elves poured into the throne room. Female elves and children elves. Soldiers flocked in too, many being stunned to see for themselves that their ruler had lied to them.

"It is a new day for the elves. I don't know how long it will take us to repair the damage you have caused, but we will try," Nalva said, pointing to the different species in the room. "We have united with others on our journey here. Believe it or not, they were already rising up to stop you. All the realms united with one common goal, to stop you. Now, together we will rebuild what has been broken.

"Leif, take some soldiers and lock him in the dungeons for now. It's far better than he deserves, but he must be held somewhere," Nalva said.

Leif turned and stretched his hand out for the dagger.

"If this is the end for me, then I am taking someone with me," Striker said with a fury in his eyes that Niv had never seen before.

He took the dagger which split into three and flung it towards Niv. Her eyes glanced to Ajax, who stood embracing Niko and didn't see the knife hurtling her way.

Suddenly something big and blue leaped in front of Nivara, knocking her off her chair.

Nivara fell to the ground and felt her chest. The daggers missed her. She pushed herself up and ran towards the blue creature and found a dagger embedded in his hind leg, one in his gut, and another high on his front leg, barely missing his neck.

She was touched that a creature that didn't know her risked his life for her.

She knelt beside him and stroked his head.

"Are you all right?" she asked.

The giant cat looked up at her. She'd never seen anything so big. The cat was about the size of an elephant. Something familiar shone in its eyes.

“Sky?” Niv asked, stunned at his transformation.

“I think after today I’m going to retire as your hero,” he groaned.

“Ajax, we need assistance over here,” Niv said, looking around. Blake had wrestled Striker to the ground and Leif tied his hands and feet.

Ajax ran over with Niko.

“My sister is skilled at healing,” Niko said. “Natty?”

A white rhino in a pale pink dress knelt beside Sky. She opened a brown satchel and took out a bottle and fresh bandages.

While Natty worked on Sky, Ajax pulled Niv to the side.

“Are you all right?” he asked.

“I am now,” Niv said.

“I should never have put my guard down until we put Striker in a cell. I’m sorry.”

“We survived, that’s what matters,” Niv said, pushing past Ajax. She ran forward and hurled her arms around Blake, who’d been making his way towards her after securing their prisoner.

“Thank goodness you’re okay,” he said, “I’ve bee—”

Niv didn’t let him finish. She kissed him.

“I love you,” she said. “I didn’t think I’d ever get the chance to tell you.”

"I think you know I feel the same," he said.

"I do. Now let's go home."

CHAPTER XXXI

Ajax

As much as they all wanted to get home, Ajax and his friends stayed another day.

Sky couldn't walk. His injuries had been stitched but he still couldn't put weight on his back leg where the dagger had gone in the deepest. Natty, Niko's sister, insisted that he rest. Ajax had asked Bolin if they'd brought any of their medicines with them, and Bolin said he'd get some to Sky.

Nalva locked Striker in the dungeon and released the troll, ensuring he'd remain captive for a very long time.

Leif spent his time getting to know his family and trying to bridge the gap between the elves. Some accepted the news of female elves and elf children with delight. Others cowered in fear, afraid to embrace change, worried that Striker would return and punish those who'd gone down a different path. A few dissenters remained, still convinced of their superior birthright.

A council would be reinstated in the coming weeks. That item of business all the elves could agree on. Having one leader make all the decisions had not turned out well for them in the past.

Mila and Ajax landed with a soft thud in front of the castle.

Ajax spent the morning helping Bolin track down Neely's family, and then Ajax paid his respects to Spots' family.

He wished his friend could see his home now, with the promise of peace.

In three weeks, leaders from every realm would be meeting here to discuss the portals. Ajax wanted to move them to more accessible locations, but soon realized that decision did not lay in his hands alone.

"Thanks for ferrying me around today," Ajax said.

"It gives me a chance to get to know this place. Once I have it down, I may have to come visit your world," Mila said.

"You'd be very welcome."

Ajax climbed the steps to the castle and smiled as elf children played outside, running past him, giggling.

The atmosphere here had changed. Species intermingled. Nalva set up a room where she could listen to creatures' grievances and try to address them. The grievance line wrapped through the passageways. It shocked Ajax how fast the word spread.

He found Nivara and Blake eating together in a large room where small tables had been set up. They had not left each other's side since being reunited.

Niv smiled as he stepped in the room, and Blake waved him over.

"We just left Sky. The medicine the merpeople brought did wonders and Natty says we can leave in the morning. She wants to watch him one more night. But he's complaining about the food not being sufficient so I know he's feeling better," Blake said.

If Sky had a dose of mermaid medicine, then Ajax knew he'd be back on his feet in no time.

"I'm not sure I like him being this big. I miss cuddling with him. I know cambriars shift shapes, but he's just not my Sky like this," Niv said, then added, "but I'm sure I'll get used to this."

A pang shot through Ajax's heart. Sky could never turn back into a hoosula. He knew a hoosula was his true fit, but Sky risked everything to save Nivara. He'd never be completely at home in any body he chose now. It would always feel off.

Ajax couldn't imagine that kind of love. He wanted to tell Niv, so she could appreciate Sky's sacrifice, but if Sky wanted her to know he'd tell her at some point.

"Are you ready to go home?" Nivara asked between bites of fruit.

"For a bit," Ajax said.

"A bit? I don't know that I ever want to leave again." Niv laughed and shoved him lightheartedly.

"I'd like to explore all the realms. I promised Neely I'd come visit. And I may need to move the portals."

"Did you ever find your medallion?" Blake asked.

He reached in his pocket and pulled it out.

"It wasn't hard. Once I removed the spell to keep it silent, I found it easily."

"But you're not wearing it," Blake noted.

Ajax shrugged. "I think I may have relied on it too much. I haven't decided if I'll wear it again." He rubbed his hand over the etching on the top.

"I would," Niv said. "It saved your life in the past."

"Well, the rest of the world survives without one," Ajax said, sliding it back in his pocket.

Niv nodded and took another bite of her food.

"Are you hungry?" she asked, raising a speared banana slice on her fork towards Ajax.

He pushed it away. "I'm fine. If we are leaving tomorrow, I ought to go and make my goodbyes."

After searching high and low, Ajax still couldn't find Leif. The castle had too many levels, and the passageways made no sense to him. Leif would never let Sky leave without saying goodbye to him first. So Ajax headed off to find him.

Sky now took up an entire bed and still his tail hung to the floor. He whined as he twisted from side to side trying to get comfortable.

"I don't like being so big," he said.

Ajax wondered with whom he conversed. From his vantage point he could see no one in the room.

"When we get back to Rastella I need to go back through the king's books and find a better body," Sky said.

"I told you, I have to stay. For now at least," the voice said.

Of course, he should have started his search here. He thought he'd find Leif here at some point.

"How's our patient doing?" Ajax asked as he made his way into the room.

"Just playing it up for attention," Leif said.

"Hey, I got stabbed," Sky said. "More than once!"

"We know," Ajax said sharing a conspiratorial look with Leif. "By the way, I've been meaning to ask you something, Sky?"

Sky looked up expectantly.

"Why did you shift forms? Why not just jump in front of Niv in your biggest hoosula size."

"I might not have been big enough, and I couldn't take that chance. I just conjured up the largest animal I could think of that I hadn't been."

"I've never seen a mountain lion this big," Ajax said, eyeing him up and down.

"Are you crazy? Do you not remember the one that tried to eat me!" Sky exclaimed.

Ajax chuckled. It seemed cambriars could not only change into animals that were not real as long as they believed them to be, but they could also distort the image in their head. Sky must have seen the mountain lion as much bigger than it actually was because of his smaller size and manifested that when he shifted.

"I hear you are leaving tomorrow," Leif said.

Ajax nodded.

"Could you do me a favor and give this to Sam?" Leif asked, pulling a letter from his cloak.

"It would be more romantic to come in person," Sky said.

Leif picked up a pillow and threw it at Sky.

"Hey, I'm injured."

"I can do that," Ajax said, accepting the letter. "You're not planning on staying here forever?"

"No," Leif said without hesitating. "I just need to make sure the council gets chosen and that things are running smoothly. I will be back to Rastella to visit all my friends."

"He just wants to see Sam. The rest of us are a bonus," Sky whispered, knowing full well that Leif could hear him.

"I may have fewer friends to visit than I thought," Leif said, and he bumped into the bed as he walked out.

"Ow!" Sky called after him.

"Enough, this relationship is too new. You can't tease him too much," Ajax said.

"Oh, I can," Sky retorted.

"I've had a long day and you look to be recovering well. I think I'll call it a day. See you in the morning.

CHAPTER XXXII

Sky

It had been many years since Sky's body had been this big. He felt awkward and off balance. He hoped his injury attributed to most of that, but he doubted it. His hind leg now only felt a little sore and tender. He no longer felt stabbing pain when he shifted positions. His neck and stomach healed completely. The medicine Bolin brought worked wonders.

He ached to be back in Rastella. He missed the simple life of living on the Maxwell homestead and Mother Maxwell outcooked anyone he'd ever met. She could do with adding a little more fish in their diet, but other than that he had no complaints.

The room he'd slept in had a small bed and a couple of chairs. Sky hopped down from the bed, careful not to put weight on his leg. Then he walked around the room a few times.

His leg felt good. It was one thing to feel fine while resting. But now that he tested his leg, Sky felt confident that they could leave today.

The stone floors felt cool beneath his paws as he made his way through the largely empty corridors. A few scattered soldiers guarded the doorways. Sky didn't think Nalva had ordered guards, but rather the soldiers did not know what to do now that Striker sat locked away in an underground dungeon.

His nose brought him to a large kitchen. Several female elves stirred big pots, while a group of children sat patiently at a table. A few elves sliced bread fresh from the oven, while others diced fruit.

"Can I get you something to eat?" a young female elf asked.

"Yes, please," Sky said.

"Just wait at the table with the others," she said, pointing.

He didn't have to wait long before elves placed bowls of eggs, sausages, fruit, and bread on the table.

After several large helpings of sausages and eggs, Sky felt adequately full. He should be able to make it to lunch now.

He made his way outside to the meeting spot they designated last night.

"Good morning, Mila," he said as he strolled over.

"Sky, is that you? I heard you'd taken a new form…so what do you think?" she asked.

Jeda, her brother, leaned forward, awaiting his answer.

"Not for me," Sky said.

"You should give it at least three months," Jeda said. "Mom always says not to be too hasty. Twelve weeks gives you time to get to know the body. To determine all the pros and cons."

"I'll keep that in mind," Sky said, then sighed as he reclined back on his haunches. He'd given up his perfect match. But he felt certain he could find something better than this. "Where are the others?"

"Here they come now," Mila said, motioning with her beak.

Sky turned to see Ajax, Blake, and Niv chatting together as they strode down the stairs.

"Do you mind if I ride with Sky?" Niv asked, turning to Blake.

"Of course not," he said, then gave her a quick kiss on the cheek.

Sky looked at the griffin as the others climbed on the animals.

"I am too big, too heavy to get on."

Niv pursed her lips and looked between the two animals. "You're right. How are we going to get you home?"

"I have an idea," Jeda said. "I will have to go get a friend to help. But I think if we wrap Sky in a blanket and tie rope around him, then with help I can carry him to the portal."

"We'll get the rope and blankets and be ready when you get back," Niv said.

Sky wasn't sure he liked the sound of this idea, but he could see no other option.

By the time Jeda returned with a large winged flying creature, Niv and Blake had wrapped a blanket around Sky's torso and then tied a rope underneath his front and back legs.

Niv brought one rope to Jeda, who scooped it up in his talons while his bird friend did the same with the rope that

Blake brought over.

"This is so embarrassing," Sky moaned from below as he swung back and forth like a pendulum when at last they were in the air.

"Don't be embarrassed. We'll find you a better shape suited for you as soon as we get back. Your bravery saved me. I don't find anything embarrassing about that," Niv called down.

Jeda and his bird friend followed behind Mila, struggling to match the pace while carrying Sky.

"Sky," Niv asked, after they'd been flying for a while.

"Yes," he said, trying to turn to see her.

"Don't answer now. I know you like the Maxwells and I don't want to put any pressure on you, but I've been discussing this with Blake and we're both agreed."

Sky waited to see if she would continue.

"I mean, if you want to. We'd like you to come live in the castle with us," Nivara finished.

Live in the castle. He'd never thought about it. When he'd been in the castle before, he had to hide. The people hadn't known about magic and talking creatures. Most hadn't even known about a portal.

Things changed in the recent months. Now everyone knew about the other realms. Sky had met other people. People he even liked. If he moved into the castle he wouldn't need to hide anymore. He could be near Niv always and still visit the

Maxwells whenever he desired.

At his current size he might be imposing on the Maxwell's hospitality. Sinda, Axel, Veda, and Edwin shared a small room. There wasn't space for him, although he knew the Maxwells would never admit it.

"I'd like that," Sky said.

"Good, me too." She laughed. "I think I missed you almost as much as much as I missed Blake."

"Now can I say I told you so?" Sky asked. "I knew you loved him."

"All right, go ahead."

A huge grin spread across his face. "I told you so," he said.

EPILOGUE

Blake

Almost three weeks had passed since Blake and his friends had returned to Rastella. The castle almost looked like it had pre-elf invasion. The resilience of the Rastellians continued to amaze Blake. They worked hard and didn't complain.

Queen Neely of the merpeople sent a hundred workers to help in the recovery. Their skills in building surpassed his highest expectations. They had also shared innovations from their land. Running water now came to the kitchens directly from a pipe. The kitchen maids no longer hauled buckets of water from the wells to cook with. Soon it would be installed inside to bathe with and launder clothes.

The king, overjoyed with Nivara and Blake's return, removed his timeline on their nuptials. They could now be wed at their own leisure.

Blake hastened his pace. He hated running late, but so many things needed his attention recently. Ajax asked them all to meet him in the library.

He skidded to a stop as he turned a corner, almost bumping into Sliver.

"Where are you headed in such a hurry?" the seer asked.

"I'm meeting Niv, Ajax, and Sky in the library and I'm running late."

"Well then I won't keep you," Sliver said, stepping aside.

"No, it's fine. I'm already late, what's another few minutes? Besides I've been wanting to talk to you. But is there somewhere you were on your way to?"

Sliver shook his head. "No, I just came from a meeting with your parents. We've been discussing portal business. I'm just on my way to see Sam now and pass on some information."

"Sliver," Blake said, shifting from one foot to another. He still didn't feel comfortable sharing his feelings but he had to do this. "I wanted to thank you, properly. You've done so much for me, for Rastella, even when we didn't deserve it."

"I have all the thanks I need. I've waited so long for the dragon eggs to hatch. I've been alone for so long." A tear spilled down his cheek. "I owe you thanks as well. This would not have been possible without your help as well."

"It was all Ajax. I didn't do anything," Blake said.

"That's not true. I've heard about your adventures from Leif, Sky, and even Ajax. You all played a part. But without each of you we wouldn't have defeated Striker and Nivara wouldn't be here at all."

Blake shuddered. "I can't even think about that."

"I won't keep you. A beautiful young lady awaits your presence," Sliver said, but he laid his hand on the prince's shoulder. "Don't sell yourself short, Your Highness. You have so much to offer, not only to Nivara but to the kingdom as well."

Blake nodded and hurried towards the library. It was hard to see what Niv saw in him sometimes when her best friend had unimaginable powers and had saved so many, but he had played his part and never gave up.

When he arrived, he saw Nivara and Ajax seated at a table with Sky lounging beside them. Sky's ears perked up and he turned as Blake walked in.

"Forgive me for my tardiness," Blake said, taking the empty seat by Nivara.

He smiled at her and she reached for his hand, intertwining her fingers with his.

"You are just in time," Ajax said, flipping open a large book with colored pages. "I found it. I knew I'd seen a picture somewhere."

"Found what?" Niv asked, leaning forward to see the image.

"Sky's new body." He pointed down at the page to an image of a black animal.

Sky jumped up, hitting his head on the table.

"Ow," he said, then leaned forward to examine the picture. "But that's a picture of a hoosula. I can't change into one again," Sky said, sounding defeated.

"No, this is a ferret," Ajax said. "There are a few differences." He pointed to the legs. "See here. Ferrets do not have extra skin under their legs. So they can scamper and jump, but not glide. And they can't shift sizes. However, as far as I can tell, it is almost like a hoosula in every other way."

"That's fine," Sky said. "I always liked my middle size best. Plus, you always gave me dangerous tasks when I shrank down to my smallest size. I will be relieved to give that up. And after being this big for so long—"

"It's only been three weeks," Niv said, poking him in his ribs.

"Well, it feels like longer. I'm ready. Ready to shed this skin," Sky said.

"Go for it, whenever you're ready," Blake said.

Sky scrutinized the image, taking in every detail, before taking a step back.

He closed his eyes and took a deep breath. Then he shook and shimmered as he shrank down and his body altered into the new form.

"Remarkable," Blake said. "You look just like your old self."

"Now this is my Sky," Niv said scooping him up and kissing him on top of his head.

"How do you feel?" Ajax asked.

"Much better."

"My apologies, but I have to leave. Well, we do. We're

supposed to have tea with the king and queen," Niv said, pushing her chair back and standing.

"Yes, it's a new tradition. A weekly meeting where we share our ideas for the future of Rastella," Blake said, offering his arm to Niv. "This is the first meeting. We don't want to be late."

Sky

He stretched his arms and his legs, reveling in his new form.

"Thank you. I was beginning to think I'd be a big clumsy cat my entire life," Sky said.

"How does it feel? The truth," Ajax said.

"It's like your mother's blueberry pancakes," Sky said.

Ajax scrunched his face up in confusion.

"I don't follow."

"Imagine your mother's pancakes. They are delicious right?"

Ajax smiled.

"Okay, now imagine them smothered in maple syrup. Even better?"

"Okay," Ajax said. "I still don't know where you are going with this analogy."

"So, when I took the form of a hoosula, maple syrup drenched me, like all over. Now as a ferret I'm just a stack of pancakes."

Ajax scratched his head. “Always food. It’s a little confusing but I think I understand. I wish I could give you syrup.”

“That’s all right. Pancakes are phenomenal after a pile of dung.”

“The mountain lion?” Ajax asked.

“See, you do understand me.”

Ajax laughed. “Can we stop with the analogies? I’m getting a headache.”

Sky spent most of the day running around, scampering through the castle kitchen, stealing the most delicious morsels and climbing trees.

His friends would be arriving at the Maxwells’ soon, so he jumped from branch to branch making his way to the homestead. It took a little longer, now that he couldn’t glide, but it didn’t bother him in the least. He’d never complain again after finding a body as close to a hoosula as this.

Squeak sat outside on the front porch curled up in a ball. It had taken Sky three weeks to get his brother outside and he still wouldn’t leave the front porch. Sky didn’t believe they’d convinced his brother that they’d locked Striker away for good. But Sky had a surprise today he hoped might change Squeak’s mind.

And Sky arrived just in the nick of time.

Jeda and Mila circled overhead.

"Down here," Sky yelled.

They landed in front of the house. Squeak hid in the corner at the sight of the griffins.

"Sky?" Mila said. She stumbled as she landed. "It can't be. How is it possible? Cambriars can't change back into a form they've already occupied."

Sky jumped up on a tree stump.

"I'm a ferret. Must be some type of cousin to the hoosula."

"So, you like being small?" Jeda asked. "Not me."

"Squeak, get over here. These are cambriars, just like us."

"Who are you talking to?" Mila asked, looking around.

"My brother. He's the small armored mouse in the corner."

At last Squeak lifted his head. "You are both cambriars?" he asked.

"Yes," Jeda said, puffing out his chest. "Have you ever been a griffin? It's fantastic, but maybe small is your size."

Squeak unrolled and scurried over, glancing up at the sky as he made his way to the tree stump beside his brother.

"Do predators attack you?" Squeak asked.

Mila and Jeda both busted out laughing.

"Who'd mess with a griffin? My beak is sharp and check out my talons," Jeda said, lifting one up and showing it up close to Squeak. "Razor sharp."

"I thought I'd like being small. That I could hide better. But I miss flying. Sky said Striker is defeated…"

"That evil elf lord?" Mila asked. "Yes, he's locked up. We've been exploring the different realms. The Mer Realm is pretty boring. It's mainly water. Not a lot to see. But this world looks ginormous."

"What do you think, brother?" Squeak asked.

"If it gets you out of the house, I think you should do it."

"If I don't like it," Squeak said, hesitating, "do you think Ajax can find me another small animal?"

"I'm sure he can."

Sky jumped off the stump, leaping out of the way as Squeak shimmered and shook, growing into a large griffin.

"A little warning next time," Sky said. "You could have squashed me."

"Forgive me," Squeak said, raising his wings and admiring his new body.

"Don't just stand there, come try those out," Jeda said, jumping up and sailing up into the clouds.

Squeak smiled at Sky and followed after him.

"Thank you. I didn't know if he'd ever leave the Maxwells' home again," Sky said.

"This world is amazing. After we bring Ajax to the meeting tomorrow, I'm coming back. There's so much to see."

Nivara

Niv's relationship with the king and queen seemed to be making some headway at last. Nivara enjoyed long walks with the queen in the evenings. The king even started to teach Niv his favorite game, chess. Blake told her that meant she had become part of the family.

They completed the construction of the new stable yesterday and her father returned to work.

Her friends were all safe. Ajax and Blake had formed a friendship, bonding over her kidnapping. She wished it could have happened without her being tortured and taken from her home. But bad things happen. At least something happy came from this one.

But now that they were home, the weight of becoming the future queen of Rastella was bearing down on her. She'd seen the power that the monarchy had and wondered if she'd be able to make the hard decisions, choices that would affect an entire kingdom. Now they had other realms to form friendships with and set up guidelines for traveling between them.

"Nivara," a voice called from behind her.

She turned to see Sliver strolling through the garden.

"How are you doing this beautiful morning?"

Her face must have given away something because before she could respond, he continued.

"Weight of the kingdom on your shoulders?"

"It's just all starting to become real. I've seen how much one person can destroy things. What if I make the wrong choice?"

"Niv, you are going to be a wonderful queen," Sliver said.

"But how do you know?"

"One, the fact that you are worried about making the wrong decisions shows you have a good heart. Also, look at what you've done with Ajax and Blake."

"Me?" Niv asked, stunned.

"Yes, your influence is calming on Ajax and Blake has tried to change because of how you've changed his view on the world."

"You always know just what to say." She wrapped the seer up in a big hug.

"Well, for as old as I am, I'd hope I've gained a little bit of wisdom."

"Thank you," Niv said.

She turned and headed towards the castle, feeling lighter than she had in weeks.

"Ajax?" Niv called as a young man strode down a corridor to her left.

He leaned back popping his head around the corner.

"Hi, Niv," he said, stepping back so she could see him better.

"You're back again, or never left?" she asked.

"Back again. I was going to come find you after. But I suppose now is as good a time as any to make my goodbyes," he said, heading towards her.

"Goodbye? You're just going to a meeting, right? I'll see you in a day," Niv said, but by the look on his face she could tell she'd been mistaken. "How long will you be gone?"

He came over and tugged on her hair, like he had done as a child. "I can't stay here. There's nothing for me," Ajax said.

"Nothing for you? How about me? Your family? Friends?"

He laughed.

"I mean, I don't really have a purpose anymore. I'm not needed. Sam is being bonded to a dragon. Sliver will train her. Then he'll pick a couple more families to be responsible for the portal. Two families aren't enough. You can't have a life when you spend most of it sitting alone by a tree. Besides, it's not a secret anymore."

He smiled and pulled out a letter with a fancy seal.

She took it and scanned it, then handed it back.

"I'm needed more elsewhere. The portals need to be moved. It will take time before everyone trusts the elves again. I can help with that. And Neely has asked for my assistance. I owe her. She did so much for me."

He reached forward and pulled Nivara into a hug.

"Besides, I'm used to adventure now. I can't just sit at home and do farm work. I want to explore. Meet new species. See everything that's out there."

He kissed her on the top of her forehead.

"And I don't think you'll need saving anytime soon."

Tears welled up in her eyes.

"So, this is it? I won't see you again?"

He poked her in the ribs.

"Of course you'll see me. I'll come back and visit. I can't miss your wedding. And as you said, I've family here and amazing friends. I just, I don't know, it's hard to explain. I feel it in my bones. I need to leave. I need to find my…thing."

"You'd better come and visit," Niv said, hitting him hard in the arm.

"Hey," Ajax said, rubbing the spot she'd hit. "You're a princess now. Look at you. You look beautiful. You'd better learn to act like one. If you hit Blake like this, he might change his mind."

"Ha. Ha. Be safe," she said, leaning forward and kissing him on the cheek.

"I will. Don't let Blake turn back into a pompous windbag," Ajax said, turning back down the corridor.

"He never acted like that," Niv said, defensively.

"Maybe not to you," Ajax said before he turned and disappeared down a corner.

Ajax

It felt like years since he had been down here. The dark passageway frightened the dickens out of him the first time he ventured down it. Now he knew where it led. A cavern of knowledge passed down from his ancestors. Now it fell to him to leave a record of his adventure in the keeper archives.

First, he found the recipe for the elixir of invincibility.

Tin kuid vinkuro hors isto sol dur

Although he still didn't know exactly what the note said, it held the key to saving them all. In his own hand below the mysterious language Ajax wrote:

It lasts twenty-four hours

Ajax's gamble had paid off. Blake defeated Striker due to Striker's own arrogance. He hoped the realms would never face such evil again, but just in case an extra note or two couldn't hurt.

He then wrote a brief account of his own story, becoming the portal keeper, entering an unknown world, and despite the hardships, coming out better for it in the end.

Tomorrow Ajax would leave. He had been invited to attend the meeting of the realms. Laws would be created and governments formed. The worlds were changing and he intended to be a part of it.

Neely sent a messenger asking Ajax to come back with her

to the Mer Realm. She needed a friend, someone she could trust for guidance, and for some reason she asked for him. Maybe he had grown up some in the past couple of years.

Ajax hadn't mentioned it to his family yet. The part that he would not be returning anytime soon. Besides, his family had their hands full.

He laughed, remembering the sight he walked in on that morning…

"Get back here," Axel yelled as he ran across the yard, chasing a green and black blur.

"Can't you keep the dragons in the barn?" Ajax laughed.

"You try. Eggs keep hatching and I can't keep up with them all. Sliver better return soon," Axel said as he grabbed the baby dragon by the spines running down his back and carried him back into the barn. "I'm just lucky they don't learn to breathe fire for several months. Can you imagine it then? Using the barn? Who came up with that brilliant idea again?"

Ajax laughed again. It had been Axel's idea. But to be fair, at the time only one dragon had hatched…

Ajax shook his head, bringing himself back to the present. His world expanded in the past year and the possibilities had no end.

Now Sliver and Sam were creating a new legacy of portal keepers. Ajax had never seen the old seer happier. The dragon kept his species safe and now a new generation of dragons was beginning to emerge. Some were already being prepared to be bonded with new human bloodlines.

Sliver even decided to stay in Rastella, which made leaving even easier. The horrors of what happened to Sliver's family and his kind on the other side of the portal made the choice easier. He needed a fresh start, and the kingdom of Rastella was giving him the welcome his friends should have received when they first visited.

Rastella's future sat secure in the hands of the future king and queen.

Leif would be visiting Sam soon, and that could only lead to more remarkable things.

And Sky…well, Sky was Sky, and he'd be here to save the day if anything happened.

Just one final task befell the sorcerer. Too much power almost destroyed him and almost cost the king his life. Sliver gave the Maxwell family an incredible gift when he bonded with their family and that was more than enough.

Someday perhaps it would be needed again, but not by Ajax.

He reached in his pocket, took out the medallion and left it on the table where he'd found it, the place that had started it all. The day he found this it altered his life, his beliefs, expanded everything he thought he knew, reunited his family, and gave him purpose. Maybe someday it would do the same for someone else.

Acknowledgements

Finishing this trilogy has been a lot of work and has taken a team of fantastic people. I count it a great blessing to have so many wonderful people who help push me to become better. Please forgive me if I miss anyone. Thank you, Casey Bell. No one could ask for a better friend or supporter. She reads all my books, sends them to her family, and comes to support me at my book events. A special thanks to my mom who edits all my drafts before I send them to my editor, so she doesn't think I'm a complete idiot. Thank you to Dawn, Kiora, and Kirk for all your feedback.

A special thanks to my editor Courtney Johansson for helping clean up my mistakes and for my amazing cover designer Meghan Edwards.

Thank you to my kids, Eden, Maximo, and Kyler for your encouragement and threats. I didn't kill Sky off, so you can all still talk to me.

Thank you, Eden, for designing Ajax's medallion. It turned out great.

Last but not least, a huge shout out to my readers. Thank you for joining Ajax, Blake, Nivara, and Sky on this journey. I hope you enjoyed it.

Don't forget to check out my blog and sign up for the newsletter to see what's coming up next.

I love to hear from readers. Drop me a line at authorstsanchez@hotmail.com.

Check out my blog: www.authorstsanchez.blogspot.com

Coming in 2023

Opened

&

Shadow Locked

CPSIA information can be obtained
at www.ICGtesting.com
Printed in the USA
LVHW081147191222
735461LV00008BB/596